DO BANANAS CHEW GUM?

JAMIE GILSON

LOTHROP, LEE & SHEPARD BOOKS
NEW YORK

Library of Congress Cataloging in Publication Data
Gilson, Jamie.
    Do bananas chew gum?

    SUMMARY: Able to read and write at only a second
grade level, sixth-grader Sam Mott considers himself dumb
until he is prompted to cooperate with those who think
something can be done about his problem.
    [1. Reading disability—Fiction] I. Title.
PZ7.G4385Do   [Fic]   80-11414
ISBN 0-688-41960-7   ISBN 0-688-51960-1 lib. bdg.

FOR LEONA GRAY

The author is grateful to Winnetka, Illinois, learning disabilities teacher Jane Herron and Wilmette, Illinois, special education coordinator Sylvia Delker and learning disabilities teacher Mary Beth Higgins for their invaluable advice and encouragement.

CONTENTS

8

1

TINSEL TEETH

IT WASN'T RAINING all that hard as I ran toward the corner office building. I could see the big letters on the silver canopy as clear as sunshine. But even after two months of glancing up at that sign, I still didn't know what it said. Not that it mattered much, so I didn't bother looking hard.

I knew my orthodontist was on the second floor. And that's where I was headed. But for all I knew the sign said _Maniac Orthodontist Inside._ I couldn't read it or any other long words without a whole lot of wheels burning rubber in my head.

See, I read like a second grader. And I'm not a second grader. I'm in sixth.

I ducked under the canopy and started to shake the rain off my leaky tan poncho when the revolving door whirled around a couple of times at about eighty miles an hour. Out flew this red-haired kid from my class at school. Wally Whiteside. He shot into me like a stone from a slingshot.

It's a good thing it wasn't into the old lady in a

wheelchair just getting out of the cab at the curb behind us. She'd have been in real trouble. I grinned to let him know it was OK, that I knew he didn't mean anything by it.

"Oh, hi, Tinsel Teeth," he said without cracking a smile.

If there's one thing I hate it's people calling me names. It makes me sick. I don't know why they can't call me just plain Sam Mott. I mean, why not? But I found out when I was in third grade that if you make a really big stink about it, kids keep it up, on and on. I lived in New Jersey then and these kids in my Penguin reading group (the slowest one) kept calling me Dumbhead Sam when the teacher wasn't looking. The other kids in the class started it, too. I kept yelling back at them, but they never let up till we moved. My dad said just forget it, but I didn't know how to do that.

By sixth grade, at least I knew enough to laugh most of the time. "Ha, ha. Very funny," I chuckled, like Wally had really laid down a knee slapper. I'd only had braces a month, but when I moved to Stockton in March, Wally was already flashing his own. "If I'm Tinsel Teeth," I told him as I drip-dried, "you must be the original Magnet Mouth. I bet you've worn them a lot longer than I have." I reached down to pick up a dime that was stuck between the cracks in the sidewalk. "Hey, good luck," I said.

When I straightened up, Wally was beaming, a pure white, metal-free, straight-teeth grin. "Just got 'em off," he said, "and I'm going straight to the drugstore to buy a huge bag of gunky caramels. A year and eight months I haven't had any candy that really grabs my teeth, and I'm dying for some." He leaned toward me and shook his head. "You know what? My mouth feels absolutely naked without traintracks."

The rain was falling much harder and it was getting crowded under the canopy. One kid who ran under had on a crazy T-shirt with an arrow on it in metallic green that pointed to the guy with him. I stared at it. It read, I'M . . . WITH . . . But I couldn't figure out the last word. Who cares? T-shirts with words on them are dumb, anyway.

"Wally!" somebody called out. This short lady with long blonde hair came running through the puddles carrying her shoes, a big red purse swinging from her shoulder. She didn't seem to care that it was raining. "Wally, you're just the person I wanted most to see," she said. But you could tell by his face that he'd have rather seen a bag of caramels than her.

She nodded to me. I must have been frowning or something because she reached up and shook my shoulder. "Cheer up. May showers bring June something or other."

"Floods," I said, staring out at the streams rushing down the gutters.

"Wally, I don't think I've met your friend," she said, smiling.

"Uh, Mrs. Glass, this is, uh, Sam, uh . . ." and Wally looked at me, blinking, trying to remember my last name.

"I'm Sam Mott," I told her. "We just moved here two months ago." I looked down to see which hand my dragon-head ring was on. I never could remember the hand to shake with so Mom bought me this ring from a kind of gum-ball machine at the grocery store to remind me. Now all I've got to do is look. I stuck out my right hand.

"Oh," she said, shaking it. "You've got good manners. I try to get my boys to shake hands, but Alex holds out his left hand and Chuckie puts his hands behind his back." She turned to Wally. "I got a job," she said. "I just now got a job. Be sure to tell your mother." She beamed at us both. "And guess what! I've got a job for you, too." She touched Wally on his nose.

"What kind of job?" Wally asked suspiciously, shifting away from her into the splash of the rain.

"I answered a 'Help Wanted' ad and got a job at the *Stockton News Advertiser*," she said, lighting up like a kid who'd just won a big panda pitching pennies. She lowered her voice. "I'm not a reporter or anything. I'll just be taking ads from one to five o'clock Tuesday through Friday. But don't you think that sounds like fun?" she asked him. "Look, I know it's a dinky suburban paper that only comes out once a week and there won't be any big deadlines or scoops or anything, but it's a real job. I'll get to talk to people all day long."

Wally was staring through the rain toward the drugstore, so she looked at me very seriously. "My husband thinks I'm crazy, but everybody I know is working. Virtually. People are always asking me, 'What do you do?' And now I'll say, 'Well, I work at the newspaper and raise two fabulous boys,' and they'll say, 'Wow! However do you manage?' and I'll say, 'It's nothing!' " She leaned down and put on her shoes. They must have made her at least four inches taller.

"I meant," Wally said, looking back at her and sighing, "what job do you have for me?"

"Oh," she said, smiling hugely. "I want you to baby-sit with Alex and Chuckie after school when I'm working. Tuesday through Friday, three to five. Chuckie will be in kindergarten all afternoon and Alex is in school all day, of course." She opened her huge red purse and took out a small calendar. "Since this is Friday, you won't need to start until next Tuesday, May tenth. I'll pay you two dollars an afternoon. Is that OK? You just meet the kids after . . ."

"Listen, Mrs. Glass," Wally said patiently, like he was talking to a little kid, "I can only come to baby-sit sometimes on Friday or Saturday nights like I've been doing. Because, see, after school I've almost always got something going." He started edging away toward the street, where the rain had almost stopped. "No kidding, like on Tuesdays I've got Boy Scouts and the rest of the week it's either swimming at the Y or, you know, stuff. Thanks a lot though. Really. I'll tell Mom about your job. See you," he said to me. And he splashed off toward the drugstore for some gluey caramel for his braceless teeth.

"Oh," Mrs. Glass said to me sadly. "I was counting on him. I really was. The boys like him because he wrestles with them and lets them win." Then she squinched up her eyes and looked at me closely. I imagined my mom saying, "Stop slouching, Sam!" so I stood up straight and smiled.

"Sam," she said slowly, like she was trying out some word she didn't know. "Sam, how old are you?"

"Twelve," I told her. "Thirteen in August." I put my hand in my pocket and rubbed the dime for luck.

"Can you baby-sit?" she asked, flinging the purse back over her shoulder. "Or do you have stuff going every day after school, too?" She was offering me a job. Me, Dumbhead Sam, a job.

I grabbed it, too. I grabbed that job so fast. I didn't have *anything* going after school *any* day and I really wanted some money. I had this thing I needed to buy.

"It would be regular work, though," she went on. "You'd have to come every day and be loyal and trustworthy and all, because I've got to work every day. I expect there are lots of mothers who'd like to get my job."

"No problem," I told her, shaking her hand again to make it legal. "No problem. Every day. Tuesday through Friday, three to five." It was like I'd discovered a cave of pirate's gold. Maybe it happened because I'd found that lucky dime.

The Glasses, it turned out, lived just down the street from me on Euclid. And my mom had wanted to get *me* an old-lady-type baby-sitter, somebody, she'd said, who could tutor me so I wouldn't have to go to any special classes like I did in California. I'd really screamed, though, and Dad had talked her out of it. "He's a big kid now," Dad had said. "He can take care of himself until we get home from work." Now me baby-sitting just down the street would really knock her out. (Ha-ha, Mom.)

I told Mrs. Glass I'd drop over Saturday to meet the boys and look around and everything and then I just whizzed through the revolving door as fast as Wally had and up the steps to Dr. Reynolds' office. Stormy day or not, it was like rainbows.

The waiting room was packed, so I was going to have to sit it out. This wire on my braces had popped loose the day before, during Social Studies. I'd tried to push it back with my pencil eraser, but that hadn't worked. The thing was drilling a hole in my cheek. That morning my mom had called and they'd said just come on over after school and Dr. Reynolds would fit me in.

I threw my raincoat on a hook and eased myself into a space on the red plastic sofa, right across from the big mirror. So there I was, looking at me. I raised my bushy black eyebrows, smiled at my reflection, and thought, You look like some lucky kid who just got a job.

It's a little weird to smile at yourself in the mirror, so I started making faces, jutting out my jaw and crossing my eyes, lapping my front teeth over my bottom lip, and pressing my finger on the tip of my nose, turning it up like a pig's snout. My hair was like a big black bird's nest, all wet and matted from the rain.

Actually, I knew this office as good as any place in Stockton. It was easy to find, right in the middle of the little business district a few blocks from home. We hadn't lived here a week before my dad brought me in to get my bite fixed. "We're going to stay in the Chicago area," he'd told me. "And this suburb will do as good as any other. This is home forever. I mean it. I'm going to take you to the best orthodontist in town and sign you up for two years of appointments for a thousand-dollar mouth of absolutely straight teeth." He'd banged me on the shoulder and said, "This time, kid, we'll stay so you can get straight teeth and really learn how to read."

Maybe we'll stay. But I doubt it. My dad always thinks that some other job is better than the one he's got. And then when he gets it he's not so sure and he starts looking around for another one. My mom calls it the Greener Job Syndrome. She doesn't like it much. Me neither. I've been to five schools since kindergarten, in five states—Ohio, Texas, New Jersey, California, and now Illinois. That's why Dad thinks it's his fault I read like a dumbhead. "I keep uprooting him," he tells people, like I'm a dandelion or something.

I crossed my eyes again and looked at the two of me in the mirror. There wasn't anything else to do. What I wanted to do was go out and run around the block—or at least look at some good pictures in *Sports Illustrated*. But a little kid with long skinny braids had already grabbed it from the magazine rack and was sitting on the floor tearing its pages out.

"Can you read that, Pussycat?" her mother asked, talking too loud and looking around, smug, like she was inviting everybody to look at her kid and think, Wow! "What's that word after 'big,' Pussycat?" she practically shouted. "I bet you know that one." I looked down at the word she was pointing at. I couldn't read it. Zero. Zip. Nothing. Blank.

"League," the little kid said, bored out of her skull, like it was the easiest thing going. (Zap! Samhead, I thought, Pussycat gottcha.)

When I was in first and second grades they said I was a "slow starter." My mom and dad argued about that a lot. They didn't like the way it sounded. My teacher in Jersey, Mr. Spears, said that I was lazy and didn't try. That *really* bugged my folks and they tried teaching me themselves and that bombed. In the middle of fourth grade we moved west. Then last year in California the teachers started asking if they could give me these tests. Geez, that was some battle royal. Finally my folks said OK, but they didn't like the test results. See, they said I had this learning disability thing. And twice a week I got special lessons from this learning disability teacher. She was helping me some, I guess. But I was still dumb. And then we moved again.

I looked hard at myself in the mirror. I decided I even *looked* dumb. Across from me on a long bench under the mirror, this girl was sitting with her mother. I knew her. Alicia Bliss. She was in Mrs. Bird's sixth grade room, too. She was new like me. Only from Arizona. And she was a real brain. At least she used big words in class and acted like she was the teacher or something every time one of her papers got posted, which was almost every day.

Alicia was really skinny. Her hair was dark, perfect, never sticking out funny or anything. It hung down to just below her ears, and when she swung her head around you could see the same little gold ball earrings she wore every day. She would have been cute, even, except she had this superior look like she knew all the answers and she knew you didn't. Some of the girls called her Miss Priss Bliss.

Mostly she didn't look at me, but when I made faces she stared. She may have been thinking how dumb I looked, too, but I think she was staring at my braces. I watched her from the corner of my eye and every time I bared my metal bands at the mirror she would run her finger across her teeth. The front ones had a space between them.

"I bet you've got a severe malocclusion of the upper mandibular palate like I do," I said, to let her know I knew a thing or two. When Dr. Reynolds had told me that was what was wrong with my teeth, I'd memorized it. Severe malocclusion of the upper mandibular palate. It sounded fatal. Everybody in the room stared at me.

Alicia raised her eyebrows and then smiled like I'd made a mildly funny joke. "Frankly, I doubt it," she said, and whispered to her mother who I was. Her mother looked up like she was about to start some kind of conversation with me, so I got up and walked over to the magazine rack again. All I could find was *Time* and *Seventeen*. *Time* is too boring and *Seventeen* is too soppy.

"Look, I'm in a real hurry," I told the receptionist. She looked at me like I was a mosquito who'd just flown into her ear.

"So," she said, "is everybody else. We'll just have to fit you in where we can."

The dental assistant leaned into the waiting room. "Mrs. Bliss, you and Alicia can come in now." I groaned out loud and the people on the sofas stared at me. They were gaping like I was some kind of freak. But I knew from experience when parents go in with you it means talk, talk, talk. Dr. Reynolds would give them the whole "Straight Teeth Are Healthy Teeth" lecture and follow that one with "What Is Orthodontia?" and "Is It Worth Big Bucks?" That meant at least another fifteen minutes.

Alicia breezed by me without saying anything.

On the wall is a poster I always look at. It's gross, really, but I can't help looking. There are these two sets of teeth. The top set is gorgeous. They look like a TV commercial for Cleaner Brighter Whiter Teeth with Dazzle fortified by New Formula Cloribrill. Then there is this other set. They are purplish gray and scaly and they look like they are about to break off at the gums. "Doesn't do any good to straighten teeth if you don't brush them," Dr. Reynolds always says.

When I can't sleep at night, sometimes I think about those scaly teeth and know that's how mine look hidden underneath my braces. When Dr. Reynolds strips my teeth somebody will probably come in with a camera and lights and take a picture to scare little kids into brushing their teeth. It might happen. You never know what's going on inside your head where it's dark and you can't see.

"Sam Mott," the dental assistant finally called from the office door.

I jumped up and followed her into the clean white office, bright with fluorescent light. Mobiles hang down above the shiny green plastic dentist's chair. The toothy smiles going around on strings and the cute bobbing kittens are supposed to make you forget all about your agony. It doesn't work.

In the next room Dr. Reynolds was telling Alicia's mother, "First, she'll need a full-head X-ray, and then an appointment for . . ." The dental assistant flipped open one of those quilted pink paper bibs and fastened it around my neck with a little chain clamp.

I leaned back in the chair and closed my eyes, feeling good about my new job, glad to be feeling good about something. Dr. Reynolds came strolling in, smelling like soap. His instruments were set up on a small round table—a mirror with a handle and a lot of little pliers.

"Got a problem here, you say?" he asked me. I opened my mouth and pointed to the raw place on the inside of my cheek. "Ah," he said, and he picked up a pair of tiny pointed pliers, reached in, and tucked the wire back in place, zip-zap. "Sometimes happens," he said, "even when you're careful." Then he handed me a thin rope of wax coiled into a small package. "If it pokes out again, just cover the end with a dab of this wax and make a quick appointment. When do I see you again, young man?"

"Wednesday afternoon," I told him cheerfully, glad to be fixed up again. Then it hit me. "Geez! Wednesday afternoon!" I groaned.

That was my second baby-sitting day. I'd forgotten all about it. "Sure," I'd told Mrs. Glass. "No problem. Tuesday through Friday from three to five. No problem. I'll walk them right home from school."

"Geez! Dummy!" I said.

"Excuse me?" Dr. Reynolds asked, unfastening the pink bib.

"Oh, nothing," I told him and slumped out of the office.

I knew my dad would explode if I canceled. All that money he's spending, he wants results. But the receptionist told me if I did cancel, the next opening wouldn't be till the *next* Wednesday. And a whole lot of good that would do me.

I stuck my tongue out at the creep with messy black hair scowling at me from the mirror and hit my head with my hand. "Severe malocclusion between the ears," I said out loud without meaning to. The people in the waiting room stared.

2

_____TREASURE HUNT_____

"Look, Reba, the kid's not going to die of it." Dad's low voice carried right under my bedroom door.

"Good Lord," Mom shouted back, "I want to know how he's going to _live_ with it."

It was Tuesday, May 10, my first baby-sitting day. I was still in bed, but I was awake. My folks think I stay zonked out until they wake me up at seven. But early in the morning is when I hear them talk about what an idiot kid I am.

"Well, Sam may not go to Harvard . . ." my dad said, trying to make her laugh, I guess.

"Harvard? Ernie, get serious. At this rate the child won't ever hold down a decent job. I hope he even makes it as a baby-sitter."

"Sweetheart, he's only twelve. It takes some kids longer to learn. You know that. I don't see why they need to draw attention to him by giving him more tests."

"Look, how do we know those California tests were

accurate? Personally, I'm glad they're going to test him again. I'm glad I signed the permission slip. And I don't know why you have to be so bullheaded. *Something* is clearly wrong with him." She turned the water on in the bathroom and shouted over the noise. "The teacher didn't seem like a total dope. She just said they wanted to find out how they could help him. So a few kids find out he's not Einstein. They'll find that out soon enough anyway."

She turned off the water and I could hear her saying low and serious, "Maybe we're just going to have to face up to the fact that he's retarded."

My dad exploded. "He's no more retarded than I am. I had a ghastly time in school, and I made it. The kid's just like me."

"Well, that's no reason for you to do his homework. It's not your grade. It's not your head."

"But it's harder stuff this year, Reba. That chapter on the Vikings isn't kid stuff. Besides, he likes it when I help him."

"You're not helping. You've got to let him work it out himself."

I closed my ears with the pillow. Through the feathers their voices sounded like a TV tuned low in the distance (*dum-dum-dum-dum*). They hadn't told me I was going to have to take tests again. I hated those tests. All those questions I couldn't answer. To keep from thinking about it I opened my eyes. The first thing I saw was the shelves across from my bed full of books, neatly stacked because I'd never read them. "Someday you'll *want* to read them, Sam," my mom always said. But I wanted to read those books about as much as I wanted to sleep with a tarantula or run the mile with my shoelaces tied together.

In a pile of orange crates next to the bookcase I had stashed all the treasures I'd found in the five states where we'd lived. My mom says I find stuff because I slouch and keep my eyes down. I don't know, but I find good stuff. Not just dimes in sidewalk cracks, either, but a ring with a red stone, amber bottles, beer cans, a railroad spike, old license plates, one watch that runs and one that doesn't, and stuff like that. My mom says it's junk, but it's my junk and I like it. It drives her up the wall.

She was always saying, "Why don't you *organize* it, Sam? Straighten it up. Make lists so you'll know what you've got." What she was trying to do was get me to practice writing, which I liked about as much as I liked to read. She really wishes I was a brain. Sometimes I bet she thinks they got the kids mixed up in the hospital when I was born.

The soft TV drone of Mom's and Dad's voices went on as I wrapped the pillow tighter around my ears. My mom, who talks the loudest, is a legal secretary.

She's going to school to learn to be a paralegal, which is harder. My dad is in public relations. Mom says she's practical and he's creative. They've got me as their only kid.

I closed my eyes tight and found a suitcase of gold bricks that a hijacker had dropped from an airplane onto a beach, breaking open an oyster that hid thirteen perfect pearls. Then Mom opened the door and called, "Sam, it's seven. Rise and shine."

The rest of the day I didn't find so good. No lucky dime, no lucky day. Mom told me Dad wouldn't help me with my homework anymore because it spoiled me. ("I rot," I told her, but she didn't laugh.) Then Mrs. Bird gave a spelling test I did so bad on I tore it up. I'd swear I handed it in and she'd think she'd lost it.

After school I met Alex and Chuck Glass by the kindergarten door, and we galloped to their house like we were horses. I wondered how they'd manage the next day with me at the orthodontist. I'd decided to wait to tell Mrs. Glass about my Wednesday appointment until it was too late for her to call the whole thing off.

I was sitting in the Glasses' kitchen trying to read this long, dumb typewritten note full of hard words from Mrs. Glass when Alex screamed, "Help, Sam, murder!" I grabbed my Social Studies book from the kitchen table, figuring to smash the rattlesnake that was swallowing him whole, and sprinted into his room.

The room was a mess. A crumpled NFL bedspread hung off the top of the bunk bed where Chuck was trying to break Alex's arm.

"Get him off me," Alex yelled. I strolled over and tickled Chuck's bare feet to break his hold. He shrieked and tumbled off his brother, giggling.

But they were at it again like bear cubs as I cruised for a good place to sit. The walls and ceiling were covered with green vine wallpaper to make it look as big as all outdoors, but it was a little room. Most of the dresser drawers were open, which made it even smaller. There was this red wicker toy box without a lid, and, thumbtacked to the ceiling, a green, dinosaur-shaped piñata with pop eyes. Pajamas, used towels, and dirty socks covered the floor, so there wasn't a whole lot of sitting space.

I decided on the rocket-print chair in the corner where Al the tiger cat was curled up, sleeping. I nudged him out and flopped down sideways. My head rested on one pillowed arm and my feet dangled over the other. The chair didn't have any slats holding up the seat, so I sank deeper and deeper.

I shuffled through the dumb Social Studies book until finally—my bottom almost on the floor—I came to this neat drawing of a dead Viking. "You two just keep playing, OK?" I told them. "I've got a test tomorrow." They stopped wrestling at once and peered down at me.

"What grade you in, Sam?" Alex demanded. "You're bigger than Wally."

"Sixth, and it's a pain," I told him. I am big. I'm five foot six, bigger than any other sixth grader, which makes me the tallest kid in school. My ears are big, my black eyebrows are bushy big, and my feet are size eleven.

"Do you wrestle?" he went on.

"Only if I have to," I said. "Now keep quiet so I can study."

Chuck flipped himself off the bed as fast as spaghetti sliding off a plate, grabbed one of my untied gym shoes, tossed it into an open dresser drawer, pulled himself up on a chinning bar in the closet doorway, and hung by his knees, arms crossed over his chest. Chuck said he wanted to be Spiderman when he grew up. I think he'll make it. His long yellow-white bangs dangled and his brown eyes gave me the upside-down evil eye.

"Wally wrestles us," he said in a funny scratchy voice, low for a five-year-old.

"You're paid to play with us," Alex declared from the top bunk. "Besides, it's raining and we're bored." Alex is in second grade, but he might be Chuck's twin. They're both skinny as Halloween skeletons. Alex says he doesn't know what he wants to do when he grows up, except it has to have something to do with dinosaurs. The kid is a dinosaur nut.

Chuck spun off the bar and barely touched the floor before he pulled off my other shoe. He tossed it in the air and the piñata lost an eye. Then he scaled the top of my chair and stared down like he was about to use me as a trampoline.

"Let's play," he said. I felt like a turtle belly-up with its shell off. It wasn't any kind of position to argue from.

"OK, I give up. Find something fabulous in the toy box." Alex crashed the red box over, dumping everything onto the floor. He dug into the jumble of up-ended toys and lifted out two fistsful of Hot Wheels cars without wheels, four broken, peeled crayons, a Snoopy scratch pad, a blue plastic baby rattle, three alphabet blocks, and a Candyland board without any pieces. It didn't look promising.

"Zero!" Chuck yelled from the top of my chair. "What's that picture?" he asked, staring down at my book.

It wasn't a bad picture, as a matter of fact. Mrs. Bird talked about it a lot in class getting us ready for the test. It shows this Viking guy laid out in a grave with one shield at his head and another at his feet. Two stirrups are spread over his legs, a really fancy engraved dagger and a two-edged sword lay by his side,

33

and in another part of the grave are the bones of two horses. Underneath this Viking they'd found a gold coin. It would have been fabulous to find all that.

"It's a Viking," I told him. I thought I'd better make it brief. I didn't know how long he could balance.

"A Minnesota Viking?" Chuck asked, amazed. "Where's his shoulder pads?" He squatted down, teetering on the chair top.

I laughed. "This guy was meaner than a million football players. He chopped people up with his sword and stole a whole bunch of gold."

"Geez," Chuck breathed. "What's he laying *there* for?"

"He's dead." I shrugged. "It's just a picture. My dad said he was found by archeologists—you know, those guys who go around digging up treasures."

Chuck brightened. "Hey, Sam," he said. "Make us a treasure hunt." And he tilted forward.

I reached up, pushed his toes off the chair, and watched him land on his feet like an inflated punching clown.

Alex shuffled through the toy heap and handed me the Snoopy scratch pad with a stubby green crayon. "You hide something and then draw us a map how to find it."

Well, look, I'm no artist. I've got to admit it. At

school I'd cut out pieces of paper and pasted them down so Mr. Kemper had said they were "interesting," but I have this very hard time making things look just right. Still, I didn't want to get fired for not playing with the kids. Mrs. Glass had said she'd give me eight dollars for four days a week and I already knew how I was going to spend the money.

I rolled out of the slatless chair and wandered into the kitchen looking for something to hide.

"No peeking," I yelled, because that's what they were doing.

The phone rang. "Glasses' house. This is the baby-sitter," I said, like I was some kind of recorded message.

"Oh, Sam," Mrs. Glass laughed over the phone. "You sound so official. That's great. Listen, what I called about was not really to check up on you or anything but to find out if the dog was dead and if Chuckie took his medicine without any trouble."

Some questions just don't have answers. I couldn't think of anything to say at all.

"Sam?"

"What dog?" I asked.

"Rooster," she said. "Rooster. I locked him in the basement all day. I never did that before, but after what he did to my rug yesterday. . . . Sam, didn't you let him up yet?"

"No, I . . ."

"Didn't you read my note? I typed it out special because my handwriting's so lousy."

"I started to, but . . ." I glanced down at the note on the table. No way, though, could I talk and read at the same time.

"So the dog is still cooped up in the basement." She sighed, annoyed. "Isn't he barking?"

"No, I . . ."

"And good grief, that means Chuckie hasn't taken his pill."

"I guess not, I . . ."

"The nurse at school gave him one at eleven-thirty. He's supposed to have another at three-thirty. It's after four. Look, do I have to come home?" She was plenty mad.

"No, no. I'll give it to him right now. Where is it?"

"It *says* in the note I typed out. It's all there. Can't you *read?*"

"Sure. Sure. I'm sorry. We just got to playing and stuff. I'll do everything right now. We'll see you around five-fifteen." I hung up, looked again at the jumble of words on the note, and felt sick.

"Alex," I yelled. "Let the dog up from the basement."

The boys barreled down the hall, opened the door to the basement, and called, "Rooster. Here, boy. Come on, Rooster." I heard scratchy paws on the steps and then this fat old brown and white cocker spaniel started running around and around my legs, yelping. At least Rooster wasn't dead.

"Chuck," I said. "Where are your pills?"

"I don't like pills," he told me, and crawled under the kitchen table.

"They're on the top shelf up there," Alex pointed, "where we're not supposed to go."

"How many do you take?" I asked Chuck as I climbed on a chair and took down a bottle from where Alex had pointed me.

"I don't take pills," he shouted at me from under the table.

"One every four hours," Alex said. "They're because last week he had an infected toe."

"Is this it?" I asked Alex. I didn't want to feed the kid poison.

"Sure, that's what it says on it, doesn't it? Chuck Glass."

I looked hard at the label. It seemed filled with print. But I think that's what it said. *Chuck Glass. One every four hours.* I was almost sure. I took one out, put the lid back on, and put it on the shelf next to the bag of marshmallows.

"As soon as you take this, I'll hide a treasure," I said.

"Chuckie, come *on*," Alex called down to him. There was a long silence, and then he rolled out from under the table, closed his eyes, opened his mouth, and stuck out his tongue. I pitched the pill in like he was a carnival game.

"OK," he said, swallowing hard, "where's the treasure?" He stuck his head under the kitchen faucet and took a gulp of water to wash the lump down.

"Scoot," I told them. "I'll come in when it's ready." As soon as they left I climbed back up and took down the marshmallow bag. There were four in it. They must have been left over from winter hot chocolate because they were stale and hard as marbles. I took them into the living room and stuck them under the pillows of the long brown velvet sofa.

Then came the hard part. I took the green crayon and drew a sort of picture of the sofa and the coffee table in front of it. I put an X on the sofa. It was an awful picture. Even I couldn't tell what it was supposed to be. You couldn't tell which side was up.

"If you don't come, I'm going to jump off the ship and drown," Chuck yelled. So I fast printed TOP at the top.

When I got back to their room the boys were standing on the upside-down toy box waiting for me. I knew it was a pirate's ship because Chuck was wearing a black paper pirate's hat with a skull and crossbones on it. It was the kind that you get at birthday parties when you're a little kid, along with a bag of chocolate coins wrapped in gold paper.

"What ho, matey?" Alex asked with a serious salute. "Have you found the buried treasure?"

"Aye, aye, sir. I ripped off the cutthroat's map," I told him, "just before I made him walk the plank and the sharks ate him, toes first."

Chuck giggled. "Gimmie," he said, grabbing the paper and hopping off the box. "Splash," he said.

I took my book out to the living room to wait while they hunted around. I could hear them arguing and whispering. Then they shot off into the kitchen, smashing around in cabinets and shuffling through the pans.

"What are you guys doing?" I yelled at them finally. "You're not hot out there in the kitchen. You're not even warm. You're cold as ice."

"Mom keeps all her pots in the kitchen," Alex yelled back.

"Why are you looking for pots?" I called.

The two boys marched into the living room, Rooster waddling behind. Alex shoved the Snoopy pad at me and pointed at my word on it.

"P-O-T spells pot," Chuck said, beaming because he could read. I looked at Alex.

"Well, that's what it says, doesn't it?" he demanded.

I looked at the pad. He was right. I'd written the dumb word backward. I used to do that a lot. It was really crazy. Then I started to laugh. Actually I didn't feel much like laughing. It wasn't funny at all, but I put on the old clown act and ha-ha-ed until the kids started laughing, too.

"Will you look at that," I said. "I must have been thinking backward or something." I forced another big ha. "That was really a dumb mistake. What I meant was *top*, not pot. See, this is the top of the page."

Geez, I hadn't done anything that stupid in a long time. I thought I must be getting worse.

"It's not a very good picture," Alex said, giving me the fish eye.

"I didn't want to make it too easy," I told him. "But I will tell you that right now you are very, very hot." I flung myself down on the sofa pillow that hid the marshmallows.

They looked at my map, looked at me, looked at the map again, tossed it on the floor, and started to search any old place. I sat and watched, thinking about how my mom was probably right that I was really a retard.

After about five minutes of crawling around on his belly, searching under lamps and plants and stuff, Chuck thought about bouncing me and lifting the cushions.

"I found it, I think," Chuck yelled. "I think I found it."

Alex ran over and they both looked at the four scruffy marshmallows. Rooster, tail wagging low, sniffed them and walked away. "Is this supposed to be it?" Alex asked, sneering. "The treasure?"

"Well," I said, picking one up very, very carefully like it was made of thin glass. "You've got to understand that this is fabulous treasure. These are petrified dinosaur eggs." I held it up high over their heads. "They're worth a million dollars each. The reason you don't see them very often is they're sweet, see, and little kids sometimes by mistake eat them—petrified shell and all."

Chuck started to pick one up, but Alex batted his hand. "What kind of dinosaur?" he asked me, testing.

"Brontosaurus," I told him. My dad used to read me books about prehistoric stuff when he was on a dinosaur kick. We even went to a museum once to see dinosaur skeletons. I bet I knew almost as much as Alex did. "Brontosaurus," I told him, "the guy with the long spiked tail."

Alex liked this game. It was his kind of game. He gave me a big wink and glanced over at Chuck. "Will they hatch?" he asked.

"Hatch? Maybe. But they're petrified, see. And at least one of them has a petrified baby dinosaur inside."

Chuck grabbed one and stuck it in his mouth, whole.

"*Give* it!" Alex yelled, furious, poking him in both cheeks. "You can't eat dinosaur eggs."

Keeping his mouth clamped shut, Chuck's bottom lip jutted out and he began to cry.

"Give me the egg. *Give* it," Alex was yelling when the front door swung open and Mrs. Glass walked in.

"I'm home early," she called brightly. "I jogged all the way in the rain. Anybody glad to see me?" She took off her dripping raincoat and hung it on a hook in the hall. Rooster danced around her feet, yipping. "Were you a bad boy?" she asked him, scratching his ears. "I was worried about you."

"Make Chuckie give the dinosaur egg," Alex wailed. Chuck stood there, mouth shut, huge tears rolling down his marshmallow-fat cheeks. His pirate hat sagged over his ear.

Mrs. Glass sat down on the living room rug and pulled the boys down with her. "Now tell me the whole story," she said to them, frowning at me like it was all my fault. She hugged Chuck, who started crunching away again on the petrified marshmallow, though you could still see the tear streaks on his cheeks. "Did you take your pill?" she asked him. He wrinkled his nose and nodded his head.

Alex gave Chuck a punch and told her about the treasure hunt.

"But that sounds like fun. Honestly, sweetie pie," she said to Alex, "it's just a game."

"He was cheating," Alex grumbled. "You don't *eat* games."

"But there are still three marshmallows left," she said, clearly irritated.

"The one he's eating," Alex said, looking Chuck

straight in the eye, "is the one with the baby dinosaur in it."

Chuck stopped chewing and started crying again.

I smiled at her very big like "Aren't they cute little rascals?" She stared at my teeth. "You like your orthodontist OK, Sam?" she asked me.

I stopped smiling. "I guess," I told her, shrugging my shoulders. "Dr. Reynolds is all right. But I think Alex and Chuck are a little young. I mean, they don't usually give you braces until you're much older—like me."

"I was thinking of much, much older—like me." She giggled. "I want to do something about my front teeth," she said. "Do you think that's silly? My husband thinks it's silly." She smiled and ran her fingers through her long blonde hair to show me she was pretty, I think. Her front teeth were crooked. Not like a hag or anything, just crooked.

"It looks to me like you've got a severe malocclusion of the upper mandibular palate," I told her.

"No kidding?" she said, frowning.

"You want your teeth to look like *Sam's*?" Alex asked, astonished, forgetting all about the missing egg.

"Oh, I don't know," she said. She looked closer at my braces. "They don't look exactly gorgeous, do they? I wonder how long I'd have to wear them? Well, I want to talk to an orthodontist anyway." She ran her tongue across her teeth. "Severe malo— Look, write his name down for me, will you, sweetie? My hands are covered with marshmallow from weepy Chuckie." She gave him another hug.

"It's Dr. *Reynolds*," I told her. "You know, his office is where Wally and me met you Friday."

"Oh, in the Professional Building. Sure. That's nice and convenient. Well, for heaven's sakes, write his name down," she said. "I won't call him right away. I'll have to think about it. Use the pad in the kitchen."

"Oh, listen, that reminds me," I told her. I had to let her know about tomorrow. "I've got this three o'clock appointment with Dr. Reynolds tomorrow afternoon. See, I get out of school a little early for it— at two-forty-five. And it's just a fifteen-minute appointment. I should get here by three-thirty at the very latest. Is that OK? Can the kids walk home by themselves? I mean, I could get another kid to come stay until I get here or something."

She bit her lip, thinking. "I don't know. Look," she said, "I'm just not sure you're up to this at all," and her eyes swept the room. The sofa pillows were on the floor. Rooster stood there wagging his tail. "I mean, you're . . ." She looked down like she didn't want to say it. "I was going to tell you. . . . When you didn't even read my note . . ."

"Please," I begged, stopping her before she finished. "I know I can do it. It was just a mistake. We were busy." I tried to tuck in my shirttail and smooth my hair.

"We're not babies," Alex told her. He thought we were just talking about tomorrow. "We'll get home at three-fifteen. So what's going to happen in fifteen minutes?"

"I could eat a dinosaur egg in fifteen minutes," Chuck said. He grabbed one and disappeared out of the room.

"I'll cancel the appointment," I told her, desperately. "First thing in the morning, I will."

"No. No, it's OK," she said finally. "OK, it's fine, I guess. For the time being. Now where's the name of that tooth straightener?"

I grabbed my book and then my raincoat from the hall, rescued my shoes from their hiding places in the boys' room, went into the kitchen, and, as slowly and neatly as I could, printed on the pad,

DR REINULDS

I ran into the living room and handed the paper to her, folded.

"Good-bye, you guys," I said, and dashed out into the rain as fast as I could, fast enough that she didn't have time enough to fire me for being stupid.

TWISTER

W<small>EDNESDAY AFTERNOON</small> I ran all the way from school just to sit and wait in Dr. Reynolds' office. He was supposed to see me at three, but it was already three-ten on the tooth-shaped clock behind the receptionist. Alex and Chuck would be home soon.

"Am I next?" I asked the receptionist.

"You are," she said brightly, "but 'next' isn't for a while."

I picked up one of Dr. Reynolds' cards from the counter and stuck it in my pocket to take to Mrs. Glass. I'll tell her I was playing a joke with the note I wrote her, I thought. Sam the Clown.

Then I grabbed a *Seventeen*, sat down on the bench, took a pencil out of my pocket, and started erasing the eyes from the models in shampoo ads. It made them look like zombies. If you erase very, very carefully, it looks like the eyes are *supposed* to be blank. With totally white eyes, this glurpy girl looked like the walking dead. Turning the pencil around, I drew her

46

eyeballs back in—black dots staring in opposite directions. It was a masterpiece. I felt wonderful. Best art I'd ever done. Holding the picture out, I smiled at it with pure pleasure.

I was still rubbing away, almost to the back of the magazine, when the hall door opened and a kid walked into the waiting room. He lifted the magazine out of my hand and sat down next to me, running his fingers through his curly red hair and showering me with water.

"Hey, Tinsel Teeth," he said, "I thought you sat on babies after school today." Wally's yellow slicker drooled water on the bench, the rug, the magazine, and me. "It's raining like crazy out there. Again! I just saw two elephants walking down Willow Street. And behind them were two skunks and two snails."

"What are you and your naked teeth doing here?" I asked him, grabbing the wet magazine back.

"Yeah, naked," he said, taking the pencil from me and drawing lines like wires across the crazy-eyed model's teeth. He stood up, hung his coat on a hook, and shook his head like a dog does to dry itself. "Listen," he whispered as he sat down on the wet puddle his coat had made. "I'm getting my dumb retainer today."

"Geez, those things are a pain," I moaned. "What's it really like?" I asked him. "Does it hurt?"

"Got me. It's this pink plastic thing with wires that

fits on the roof of your mouth." He poked his thumb up onto his palate. "Ike iss," he explained, tilting his head back. "My sister's got a retainer and she's always taking it out at the dinner table. It's gross. Anyway, it's supposed to keep your teeth from going crooked again. I've got to wear it a year or something."

"Too bad."

"Yeah, but I can take it out at least and eat caramels." He took a caramel out of his pocket, slowly unwrapped it, and popped it in his mouth. It was golden brown and nutty. "Want one?" he said with an evil laugh. "Speaking of torture, how'd you do on the Viking test?"

"I don't know," I told him. "I don't think I totally blew it. I did pretty good on the true-false and the multiple guess. It was the essay part, though. I really did blow that. How about you?"

Wally shrugged his shoulders. "I couldn't remember all that junk about Eric the Red in Iceland and wherever else he went," he said.

"Sam," the dental assistant called, and I jumped.

The minute I sat down in the green reclining chair I thought about calling Chuck and Alex. It was black as night outside and raining like mad. Maybe the kids were scared.

"I've got to get out of here fast," I told the dental assistant as she clamped the pink paper bib around my neck. She left just as Dr. Reynolds came in.

"Shall we just tighten these up a bit?" he asked, tilting the chair back and picking up the mirror. He flipped the light on and tipped it down from my eyes to my mouth. Moving in fast, he unfastened the wires, drew them out, snipped three new lengths of shiny wire from a big wooden spool, and then threaded them zip-zap through the holes. The ends of the wires stuck way out—about three inches—on both sides of my mouth. I felt like a wire-whiskered cat.

"Telephone, Doctor," the receptionist called. "Can you take it?"

"Sure," Dr. Reynolds said, patting me on the shoulder. "It's all right with you, isn't it, young man?"

"Og," I said, my mouth filling up with saliva.

I wondered what it would be like if Dr. Reynolds by mistake laced my top and bottom teeth together. That's what they do to fat people so they can't eat french fries and double chocolate brownies. I put my hands up to feel the edges of my antennas, and hissed like a black-eyebrowed panther.

The dental assistant breezed in and over to the window. "Well, would you look at that sky!" she said, and I looked. Even with the bright light in my eyes I could see it wasn't just plain dark anymore. It was weird dark —a yellow-green like split pea soup. "I don't like the way that looks at all," she said, hurrying out.

I could see into another office across the street where the lights were on and two women stood at the win-

49

dow pointing up at the strange sky. The linden trees that grew out of round holes in the sidewalk were whipping around in circles. Hailstones began to pelt the windows like BBs.

Alex and Chuck are scared, I thought, squirming around in the chair. I should have waited at school and brought them to the office with me.

"*Wowoooooooowooooooowooooooowooooooo*," the sirens outside began to howl over the wind.

"Oh, darn," the dental assistant sighed, coming in again to check the sky. "Tornado warning. Just when we're running so far behind. I always feel like such a fool," she said, "hiding in the hall when those things go off. It's one chance in a million a tornado would hit. Maybe a billion. Well, we better move it."

"*Woooooooooowoooooooooooowoooooooowooooooo*," the siren blasted again. A dark cloud dipped down from the pea-green sky and a thin gray film broke away and swirled off toward the north. I leaned forward to see the trees across the street bend low. The window shivered like it was as scared as me. I leaped out of the chair, wires flapping, and ran like crazy for the hall.

"*Wowoooooooowooooooowooooowooooo*," the sound of the siren outside followed me.

The small gray sirens on the hall ceiling looked like toy horns, but they blasted like trumpets. "*Wahwah-wahwahwahwahwah!*" People rushed out of all the doctors' offices along the hall, holding their ears, not sure what to do or where to go.

"Sit on the floor," Wally yelled, but nobody listened.

"What's it about?" a little kid asked Wally.

"Tornado warning," he shouted back, pulling the kid down, "like at school."

I was huddled in a small knot across from them and I could see the little boy was scared. His face was the color of concrete. "It'll be all right," I shouted to him. He looked up to say something, but his eyes opened wide. He caught his breath and coughed back a laugh. Shaking his head, he grabbed Wally's arm and pointed at my mouth. My pink bib was tucked over my knees and my wires were bent up into a curly moustache. Wally laughed so hard he couldn't stop.

"Sam," he howled, cupping his hands around his mouth, "you look straight out of space."

"Wahwowahwowahwow," the siren outside echoed the blasts from the ones in the hall. It did feel like we were in a spaceship, waiting for the bad guys to explode us. If we had been on TV, it would have been time for the commercial. I grabbed my knees tighter and made a face at the little kid.

Suddenly the lights went out. And the hall sirens stopped. The dark was all at once, but the sound wound down slowly to a thin shriek. Everyone sat quiet and scared, taking deep breaths of the medicine air that doctors' and dentists' offices always smell like. Outside we could hear the wind roar like a train rushing through a tunnel—and then, from Dr. Reynolds' office, we heard the crash of glass.

We sat quiet, just feeling our hearts beat for maybe five minutes. I imagined that my house had been blown away and that Alex and Chuck had gone running outside and been blasted away up into the sky because I wasn't there to hide them. My hands were sweating and my ears felt like they were going to explode. I had to yawn to make them stop vibrating.

It was still dark in the hall when the all-clear sounded outside. Everybody scrambled up, feeling their way down the rough stucco walls of the hall and back into offices where there were windows. I was afraid I'd knock somebody down if I ran, so I crawled to the end of the hall where the steps were and skidded down them like a seal at the zoo.

I guess everybody else wanted to be super safe because I was the first one outside. There weren't any buildings down, but the street was a bathtub of water and the windows of the travel agency next door had blown in.

I ran like a rocket toward the Glasses' house. Branches were scattered everywhere like pick-up sticks. The telephone in front of the grocery store was swinging back and forth off its hook. Up ahead a light pole tilted, though the wind had died down and nothing was blowing it. I ran fast, panicked about the kids.

"Hey, son, watch it," somebody shouted. I turned to see the pole bending down closer to the ground, aiming itself at me.

"Over here!" It was a policeman, his car up to its hubcaps in water. As I dashed toward the squad car I could hear a long low crack, and when I looked again I saw the pole scrunch the top of a parked car, blocking the street. A shower of sparks flew up like fireworks. I turned to run again and tripped over the lid of a trash can that had blown like a flying saucer into the middle of the sidewalk. It sent me sailing, too. The concrete sandpapered the skin off my hands. My pants and shirt were soaked.

"You OK?" the policeman in the squad car yelled. I shrugged my shoulders.

"How bad is it?" I asked him.

"Dunno. Two funnels dropped down. Some damage over on Euclid Avenue, I hear. More wires down over there, too. Stay away from Euclid now, and go right home."

"Euclid *is* home!" I shouted back and started running again. The Glasses lived just two blocks away from my house on Euclid Avenue. What if . . .

My skinned hands hurt. No Band-Aid was going to be big enough to cover those scrapes. But I ran like crazy.

What kind of damage was there? Why didn't I ask

the policeman? Were the houses blown to toothpicks? The closer I got to Euclid, the worse it looked. More wires dangled from tilted poles, sparks showering each time they touched the wet ground. A fat limb blocked off the street and a police car trying to get through had to turn around to look for another way. I could hear the siren of a fire truck in the distance. But I kept running.

The street was blocked again with a car lying on its side. I ran over to look, afraid somebody might be inside, bloody or dead or something, but it was empty.

An old guy with a cane came out on his front porch. "Is it safe now?" he shouted, waving his cane at me. I didn't have any breath to call back so I nodded my head yes. After I passed him, I thought, You stoop, that's a lie. All those wires down. It's not half safe. Stuff had been scattered around near Dr. Reynolds' office, but nothing like my street. It looked like it had been caught in a blender. A big pine tree was blown over, a smashed-up doll carriage in its branches like a Christmas tree decoration.

My house was still standing, but the chimney had fallen off. Bricks littered the yard. I didn't stop to check inside. Mom and Dad were both at work so nobody was home. I steamed ahead to look for Chuck and Alex.

I got there just when Mrs. Glass did. It's a good mile from the newspaper, so she must have done some running, too. She came sailing down Ninth Street over to Euclid, splashing through puddles, her high-heeled shoes in her hand.

"Sam," she called to me. "Where are the boys?"

"I don't know," I admitted. "I just got here." I took the steps two at a time. The front windows were broken in. I flung open the door. Shattered glass lay scattered on the living room rug and all over the brown velvet sofa where I'd put the marshmallows.

"Alex!" I yelled. "Chuck! You OK?"

Nothing. Zip. Silence.

"Chuckie!" Mrs. Glass screamed. "Alex!" I dashed around the house, searching. Something moved in the top bunk so I scrambled up the ladder, sure I'd found them. But just as I got to the top, Al the cat leaped down.

"Go find the boys," I yelled at him. He stared at me for a minute and then settled in the rocket-print chair to watch.

Mrs. Glass opened the basement door and shouted, "Boys! It's safe now." Only Rooster scrambled up the steps. Dashing into the hall, I ran smack into Mrs. Glass, who was dashing someplace else. It almost knocked us both flat.

"Maybe somebody rescued them," she said. "I don't see any blood. The phone's dead. The electricity's off. The windows are blown in and the old maple tree in the backyard is roots up." She started biting her nails.

"The place is a disaster area." She looked at me, glanced away, and then looked back again like she just couldn't believe her eyes. "And you," she said, "look like you're going to a costume party. Where were you all this time, anyway?"

"I was curled up in the hall outside Dr. Reynolds' office," I told her. "He was running late. I know I should have . . ." Then I looked down at my mud-spattered pink bib and put my skinned hands up to feel the curly metal whiskers. I'd forgotten all about them. "Dr. Reynolds had just put in my wires . . ." I started to explain.

"Reynolds?" she said. "Was that the weird word you tried to write?" Then she frowned, closed her eyes, and shrieked as loud as all the sirens at full tornado force, *"Boooooooooyyyyyyyyyss!"*

From their bedroom I heard a faint whimper and an almost silent "shhhhhhhh." I ran in and threw open the closet door, but only shoes fell out.

So I got down on my belly, lifted the NFL bed-spread, and looked under the bed. My old finding powers hadn't left me. There among the dirty socks and dust balls lay Alex and Chuck, scrunched up small against the wall, looking gray and scared.

"I found them, Mrs. Glass," I yelled. "They're alive!" I stuck my head under the bed again. "It's all over, you guys," I told them. "You can come out now."

"Alex turned it on!" Chuck yelled from deep under the bed.

"We didn't mean to do it," Alex whispered in a weak, dry voice.

"Come out here this minute!" their mother boomed.

Chuck poked his head from his hiding place. His bottom lip was quivering. "Alex did it," he cried. He slithered out, ran over, and clung to his mother's knees.

"Alex did what?" She tried to pry him loose so they could carry on some kind of conversation, but he hugged fast.

"Alex, come out!" I told the dark form pressed against the wall.

He inched toward me, peering at my face with interest. "What's wrong with your mouth?" he asked.

"It's a long story," I said, tearing off the pink bib and tossing it over toward the wastepaper basket.

"What's she gonna *do* to me?" Alex hissed.

I stuck my head under the bed. "She's going to be *so* glad to see you," I said, trying to grab him by the leg, "that she'll give you a big hug and a kiss."

"Yuck," he said. "No kidding, what's she gonna do, you think?"

"Alex," Mrs. Glass said in a low threatening voice. "You're going to die of dust inhalation if you don't get out of there." She shuffled toward the bed, Chuck clinging to her knees. Alex sneezed and shifted back toward the wall.

"What is the matter with that crazy kid?" she asked nobody in particular.

"You've told him a billion times not to play with Daddy's stereo," Chuck said, sniffling, "but he did and . . ."

"I'm going to get you, Chuckie," Alex shouted from his cave. "Next time you beg me not to, I'm going to rat on you. You'll see." And he started to sob.

But Chuck kept going. "And he turned it up so loud the house started shaking, and it shook so much it exploded, and my ears hurt and the lights went out and there were noises outside . . ." He started to wail.

By then it was Tear City. Mrs. Glass was doing it, too. She burrowed under the bed, dragged Alex out by his foot, and they all three of them sat there and bawled. It was catching. I almost started in with them. I mean, really it was *my* fault because I wasn't with the kids. Maybe if I'd come home with them or at least called them the storm wouldn't have happened that way. It was my fault as much as anybody's.

"*You* didn't do it, you funny nuts," Mrs. Glass said. "It was a tornado from the sky. You know, like that funnel cloud that picked Dorothy up in *The Wizard of Oz*."

Geez, what a dumb thing to say, I thought. Next

time they'll run out and try to catch a ride to the Emerald City.

"Well," she laughed, smoothing the dust balls out of Alex's hair, "I'll bet it's a couple of light years before you fool with Daddy's sound system again."

She bounced up, fluffed her hair, and smiled down at the two kids, who looked like they'd been personally responsible for losing the World Series. "Let me fix some popcorn to cheer you up. Sam, read to them, will you? That's the best soother I know." She handed me a book with a duck on the cover.

I opened it to the first page. I could feel my brain frost over. Mrs. Glass was waiting.

"Oh, Mother Goose, good," Chuck said. "Do this one," and he flipped the pages to a picture of a little girl talking to a hunched-up old man.

"Mother Goose, yuck," Alex groaned.

"One . . . one . . ." I said, then looked again at the picture. It didn't give me any hints at all. I don't know why, but it's hardest for me to read out loud with people watching and listening. My thinking stops like a faucet turning off. "Once upon a time," I said, faking it.

"Dummy, that's not a 'Once upon a time.'" And Chuck rattled off by heart,

"One misty moisty morning when cloudy was the
  weather,

59

There I met an old man clothed all in leather.
He began to compliment and I began to grin,
'How do you do,' and 'How do you do,' and 'How
   do you do again.' "

I laughed like I was Bozo. "Can't fool you, can I?"
I said, like it was some classy joke I'd pulled on him.
"Probably it's my metal whiskers." I curled them up,
stuck out my tongue, and crossed my eyes—Sammo, the
clown.

"You're crazy," Chuck said, laughing. "Sam's crazy."

Mrs. Glass gave me a long funny look. "I want to
talk to you later, Sam," she said, like she had important things to say. The frost that had hit my brain
moved to my stomach.

"Sure," I told her. "Anytime. But listen, is it OK
if I go home now? I want to see if my house is still
there and everything."

It was getting lighter out. From the boys' window
we could see that a porch had been completely sheared
off the house next door. A whole batch of people had
gathered round, waving their arms to show how the
tornado had totaled the place. And out in back we
could see the Glasses' huge tree, uprooted, like some
giant had thought it was a weed and pulled it right
out of the ground.

"Can we wait and talk tomorrow, Mrs. Glass?" I
said, figuring if I worked one more day I could earn
at least two dollars more before she fired me. She

couldn't very well pay me for today. All I had done was flap around.

What I wanted the money for was to buy a tape recorder to take to school. Just a little one so I could hide it. Mrs. Bird was lecturing to us, trying, she said, to teach us to take notes. But when I tried to write things down I missed half of what she said. My paper would be all crossed out and scribbled over and smudged. And I wouldn't even have heard half of what was going on. It was a big mess.

The teacher in California told me I should take a tape recorder to school. Mom said absolutely no I couldn't have a tape recorder because then I'd never learn to read hard stuff or write so "normal people" could read it. But I wasn't learning anyhow. Dad said why not, but I'd have to earn the money myself. Being dumb is no fun.

"I'll stay longer if you really want me to," I told her, looking down at the holes in the toes of my gym shoes.

"No, Sam, I guess you do want to go home and check," she said. "Call me if you need help. You know our number?" She wrote it on a scrap of the old Snoopy notepaper and handed it to me.

"824-1276," I read off. "And they add up to 30. Right?" I knew it was right. Numbers are no problem to me. (Ha-ha, Mrs. Glass. Ha-ha.)

"See you tomorrow," she said, without a smile. "And don't be late."

4

THE GREAT CAFETERIA DIG

"I'D LIKE TO SEE YOU for a while after school today, Sammy," Mrs. Bird said, lowering her voice as she stopped at my desk. She'd been sailing up and down the aisles snooping over our shoulders as we wrote. I snapped the tip off my pencil, then lifted the desk top so I could search through the mess inside for one that still had lead. Marching across the room to sharpen it would be a pain. A short yellow tooth-marked one was stuck inside the math book. I took it out, shifted around in my seat, and covered my paper with my arm so nobody could look. My stomach growled. I felt like growling, too.

We were supposed to be doing creative (ha) writing about the big twister of the day before. I had a whole lot of stuff in my head about it and a whole lot of wild words my dad had used when he got home and saw the mess, but all I'd gotten down was:

THE TWIZTER BY
SaM Mott I RaN fROM
ofise To Halpth KIDS.
I saw a tól fall I
saw sptrx in AIR.
A MaN askt Me if
it was saf. I saD
Yes But It was
relly DanGerus IT
was

It took me half an hour to do that much creating (ha). I stared out at the sky, which was bright blue with cotton candy puffs of clouds floating in it. The tops of the trees on the lawn across the street almost touched the clouds. I thought about the huge tree lying flat in the Glasses' backyard and how the boys and me could climb it after school and how great it would be to jump around in the high limbs of a tree and know you couldn't even fall and break a leg. I wondered what lunch would be. Tacos maybe.

Across from me Wally was filling pages up with paragraphs. Once he held up his paper to show me. He'd drawn a picture in the margin of me and my metal whiskers.

Just so anybody who looked would think I was writing, I added at the bottom of my page, "DUM DUM DUM ME DUM ME."

Mrs. Bird probably wants me to finish this after school and it'll take a year, I thought, and Chuck and Alex will *really* have blown the house apart by the time I get there.

"I've completed mine, Mrs. Bird," Alicia Bliss said brightly, raising her paper in the air like it was the Statue of Liberty's torch. "Is there anything I can do for you?" A girl in the next row hissed, "Priss is at it again."

The hands of the clock snapped shut to twelve and the lunch bell rang.

"Pass your papers up to the captains, people," Mrs. Bird called from the front of the room. Our class was made up of People, Captains, and the Bird, who'd elected herself General. The kid first in every row was a captain. Alicia was mine. She turned around and smiled at me, sweet as Sugar Pops.

The last thing I wanted to do was let a brain like
that know I was some kind of idiot, so I stuck the
paper in my pocket and raced out the door.

"Don't leave until you hand in your papers, people," Mrs. Bird commanded.

Wally was at my heels. "Hey, what happened to
your steel whiskers? Lightning strike them on the way
home?"

"No," I told him as we got our stuff from our
lockers, "Mom unthreaded them while Dad swore at
the chimney. The whole top part of the crazy chimney
flew off and some of the bricks crashed through our
neighbor's window and broke the screen of his TV
set. My dad says it was an act of God. But our neighbor says our chimney needed tuckpointing and if it
had been in better shape it wouldn't have happened.
My dad says they're crummy neighbors and maybe we
should move."

"Nothing happened to our house," Wally said with
a sigh.

We ran, skipping steps on the way down because
there was nobody to stop us.

The grades eat in shifts, the little kids first, and
most of them were still there, poking at their sandwiches. Outside the sun was shining, but inside it was
even brighter. Our cafeteria is caution-yellow with
pictures of street signs stenciled all over it—*One Way,
Stop, Merge, Yield*.

"Walk!" a teacher yelled at us. "Walk! There's food aplenty."

The cafeteria smelled like sack lunches and bananas. And french fries. No tacos today. It sounded like somebody'd stuck a microphone into a beehive and turned the volume all the way up. But I was starved so it didn't matter. The line shuffled along slow.

Some third-grade girls just finishing their desserts were trying to get the gym teacher, Mr. Bromfield, to notice them. Mr. B. cruises the cafeteria every lunch hour to keep order.

"Mr. Bromfield, Mr. Bromfield, my mother made some ginger snaps. You want one?" a kid in a Girl Scout uniform called.

"Not now," he said, and bounded over to stop two first-grade boys from stomping on upside-down paper cups.

We looked at the trays as the kids filed past. Hot dogs with pickles on the side, french fries, and chocolate milkshakes in paper cups.

"Looks good," I said, my stomach growling because I'd only had a piece of toast with peanut butter on it for breakfast.

"Good?" Wally sneered. "You gotta be kidding. You know what's *in* those milkshakes? My mother's in the PTA and she says they've got ground-up brown kelp in them for vitamins. Seaweed! I'm not gonna drink any seaweed milkshakes."

"They taste all right, though. I remember they taste like chocolate."

"Maybe, but it's like eating rattlesnake. Doesn't matter if it tastes good. I wouldn't touch it. Not even with chocolate."

A bunch of girls in line behind us were trying to top each other with storm stories. It sounded like everybody had been *almost* drowned or electrocuted or smashed by a falling tree or speared by glass missiles.

When we got our lunches, I took a malt and Wally took a milk. He rolled his eyes at me and gagged.

The only free table was a four-seater across from the trash smasher—a table with a view. But it was all there was, so we grabbed it.

A big white plastic garbage can yawned out in front of the trash compacter. The little kids, just finishing their lunches, were emptying stuff into it, sloshing leftover milk and milkshakes into the garbage can and tossing the rest into the compacter. Then they plunked their mostly empty trays on top of the tray pile.

"Hi, Sam!" Alex came up behind me and pushed his tray under my nose. "Hi, Wally, wanna wrestle?"

"How you doing, kid?" I asked him, pretending not to notice that his tray swam with malt, hot dog, and dead french fries.

He smiled. His mouth was ringed with chocolate malt. "My dad found an exploded basketball in our backyard," he said proudly. "My dad says the volcano must have busted it."

"Tornado," I told him, grinning at Wally. "Meet you and Spiderman at the kindergarten entrance at three o'clock sharp. Same as Tuesday."

As he walked away Alex said proudly, "When the electricity came on, the stereo was so loud it nearly knocked our ears off." He wiped his malty moustache on his sleeve. "My dad wasn't home yet, though, so it was OK."

"Sitting them is a total riot," Wally said. "My mother thinks their mother is a total flake, though. They bowl together." Then he shifted his eyes back and forth to see that nobody was looking but me, reached in his mouth, and lifted out his new retainer. It was all pink and wirey. He looked for a place to put it.

"It's gross. I know it. I've got a pink plastic box I'm supposed to stick it in. I left it home, though. It'd be such a pain to carry it around all the time. But I found out you can't taste a thing when the retainer's in your mouth," he whispered. "You've *got* to take it out." He tucked the retainer under some french fries just as this other kid from our class, David somebody, sat down with us.

A pack of girls from our class grabbed the big round eight-chair table that had just emptied out next to ours. "Here comes Miss Priss," one of them hissed. "Why doesn't she just sit with the rest of the teachers? Quick, throw your coats on the empty seat."

There was a rustle of jackets and then suddenly a crash and a shriek as this girl came sliding across the floor, her tray skidding out ahead of her.

"OK, now, who's the wise guy?" Mr. Bromfield hurried over to see who'd tripped her. The girls at the other table stared away as though this kid hadn't flopped on the floor right under their noses and flung her french fries halfway across the cafeteria.

He eyed us. "*We* didn't do it," David said.

It was Alicia on the floor, all right. She rose up to her knees and pointed at the girls sitting at one side of the big table. "Mr. Bromfield," she said in a high, shrill voice, "one of those girls is *obviously* guilty."

I didn't know if she was going to cry or what. She was pretty upset, especially because the girls went on talking, pretending they hadn't seen or heard a thing. I guess Alicia could see nobody was going to confess, so she got up, put her hands on her hips, and said, "Mr. Bromfield, it is *imperative* that you punish them!" Her voice quivered. She walked over and stood next to the girls who might have done it. "I will not be made a fool of," she said, like she was an actress or something.

The girls couldn't ignore her anymore. She was practically standing on top of them. First they glared at her. Then, when they couldn't take it any longer, they broke out in giggles.

Mr. B. wasn't sure what to do. "Girls," he said, "is it possible you are responsible for this?"

They tried to hold back their giggles and it sounded as if they were all about to sneeze. "Obviously not," one of the girls on the aisle managed to say straight-faced. "She must have tripped on her feet."

Alicia whirled around, limped over to the upset tray, leaned down, and picked up her green purse with a gold chain.

Mr. B. hurried off to round up a janitor to clean up the mess.

"You OK?" I asked Alicia.

"No!" She narrowed her eyes at the girls, marched back through the cafeteria line, and then headed straight toward us with a new tray of food. For a minute she stopped behind the chair piled with jackets at the girls' table, but brushed past it and put her tray down between David and Wally.

"May I sit here?" she asked.

Wally's face flushed like he'd fallen asleep in the August sun.

David looked the other direction. She was biting her lip and I knew doing that kept you from crying.

"Sure," I told her. "Be our guest." I mean, why not? It wasn't her fault, really.

70

"Who's your girl friend, Wally?" somebody at the next table called. They all giggled.

"I, um, see, I've got a kick-ball game right now . . ." Wally mumbled, not even looking up at Alicia. He grabbed his tray, dumped it into the compacter, and fled to the playground.

David ran with him, leaving Alicia and me at the table alone. She sat up very straight and didn't say a thing. I don't know why but I just couldn't leave her all by herself. The girls got bored with teasing and turned away.

We watched Mr. Westfall, the janitor, push the button that made a big metal plate smoosh all the garbage into a neat cube. He lifted it out, fastened the top of the plastic bag it was in, put it on a cart, and rolled it away.

And just as he had finished fitting a new bag in place, Wally came flying into the lunchroom.

"I've lost it. My mother's gonna kill me. She told me I'd lose it if I didn't take that dumb pink holder. Geez, I bet it cost about a hundred dollars."

We stared at him.

"My retainer's in there," he said, pointing at the compacter. "It's in that machine with all the seaweed malt cups and french fries."

"No, it's not," Alicia said.

"Yeah, yeah, it is. I threw it in myself. I remember." He stared at the big machine and pounded his head with his hand like he wanted to knock out the incredibly stupid thing he'd done.

"It is not," Alicia said.

He looked at her suspiciously.

"Mr. Westfall compressed it and carted it away," she went on. "It's not there."

Wally turned green. "He *smashed* it?" Then he looked at me to tell him it wasn't true.

"Yeah," I said, nodding my head. "We watched him smash it."

"Well, why didn't you *stop* him?" Wally yelled.

"Look," I said, trying to calm him down. "Maybe it wasn't totally smashed. Besides, we didn't even know it was in there. I'll help you look for it if you want me to." I figured the longer it took me to get back to class, the better off I'd be. Even garbage picking would be better than having the Bird bug me about that paper. I'd take it home, hoping that maybe Dad would help while Mom was still at school and didn't know any different.

"Yeah, but where *is* my retainer? It isn't already in some dump someplace, is it?"

"Got me," I said.

"You might ask Mr. Westfall." Alicia swept her hand over toward the janitor at the other end of the cafeteria. She was in charge again.

Wally sprinted away until Mr. B. called, "Walk," and then he walked very fast. But by the time he got back he wasn't green anymore. He was ketchup red.

He sat down next to me and leaned over to talk in my ear. "It's in the garbage room," he mouthed. Alicia moved closer. "Mr. Westfall says it happens all the time—people throwing away retainers and stuff. He says the kid who loses it, though, has to scrounge around looking for it. No way, he says, *he's* gonna do it." He shook his head. "I've never heard of anybody pawing through the lunch garbage, have you?"

"It's probably one of those things people don't broadcast," I told him.

"Where *is* the garbage room?" Alicia asked crisply, like she was supposed to be part of the conversation. "We'd best begin or we'll be late for Social Studies."

Wally's eyes opened wide.

"You don't need to help," he said, glancing over his shoulder to see if the girls were listening. But they had long since gone outside. We were almost the only ones left. "I don't want you to help."

"I don't mind," Alicia told him. "Besides, before we moved here my mother told me, 'Alicia, help out all you can and you'll make friends.' Not that it turned out to be very good advice."

Wally edged away.

"Oh, come on," she said, sounding almost real. "I clearly haven't got anything else to do. The girls won't even *talk* to me. Please."

"Oh, I guess OK," Wally told her. "But listen, don't go telling anybody. OK?"

The cooks showed us the garbage room behind the

kitchen and told us not to mess it up. We could have used some paper clips for our noses. Boy, did it stink. It was painted tornado-sky green, and it was piled up in back with old globes and workbooks and plastic cans emptied of copying machine gook. In front were three bags of squared-off garbage sitting side by side, each about two by two feet of stuff to search through.

"All right, then, which one's it in?" Alicia asked, hands on hips, ready to plow in.

"He said he couldn't remember which sack he put in last. We'll have to look in all of them," Wally told us, stepping back outside to take a deep breath.

"Don't be an infant," Alicia told him. "Garbage men get used to smells a lot worse than this."

"It's not as bad as sauerkraut," I said, trying to think of what could be worse. "Or the zoo, sometimes."

"We'll each take one," Alicia said, carefully untying one of the plastic bags, "unless you prefer to just forget about the whole thing."

Wally gulped some kitchen air outside the door and then dashed in and tried to untie his bag fast while he held his breath.

Alicia started shifting things around in the bag she'd opened. "Eureka!" She held up a quarter and two dimes. "Treasure!"

Wally's nose suddenly got less sensitive. He tore open the bag he'd been picking at and started digging.

"Look at this," he called, lifting out a purple Road-runner lunch box, only slightly dented. "How could anybody be so stupid as to throw away something like this?"

Alicia just looked at him and raised her eyebrows.

"Well," he said, turning away, "maybe the kid was in a hurry. Let's save the good stuff over here." He put the lunch box next to the door and eyed the forty-five cents. Alicia smiled and put it in her purse with the gold chain.

"I think I'm earning it," she said.

I opened my bag and started looking for clumps of french fries. I remembered that's what he'd hid the retainer under. And it had to be nearer the top of the pile than the bottom because it wasn't too long after he'd left that we'd watched the janitor cart it away. The stuff wasn't really packed tight like those cars that get cubed, so it wasn't all that hard to shuffle through.

"Hey, my turn," I said, flashing a slightly damp blue folder. "Here's somebody's report! Doesn't have a grade on it, so it must not have been handed in yet." I laughed. "Somebody's teacher's not gonna believe it got swallowed by a hungry trash smasher."

"What's it on?" Alicia asked.

"Fresh something," I told her, glancing at it. I put it down behind me. "I'll turn it in at the office."

She reached over and pulled it away. "Fresh noth-ing," she said. "It's on the French Revolution."

I shrugged my shoulders. "So?" I said. "Who cares?" Unless I *want* to I don't even try to read words that look hard. Idiot. Dumbhead! "Geez, these kids waste a lot of food," I said fast and loud to Wally. "I bet I've gone through a thousand french fries. Some of these sandwich bags haven't even been opened."

The bell rang. Everybody outside would be heading in to class.

"I'll run and tell the Bird what we're doing," Wally said, getting up and easing out the door. "Can I leave you two alone?" He winked at me and fled through the kitchen.

"You're all heart, Wally, all heart," I called. "You go on back to class," I told Alicia. "I don't want you to miss anything."

Alicia stopped digging. "Oh, I can afford to miss. I'm already doing next week's work. That's what makes the girls so mad. They're jealous. I guess geniuses are always lonely." She sighed, closed up her garbage bag, and leaned against the concrete block wall. "I don't care, of course. I understand them. I'm going to be a psychiatrist when I grow up. Like my Aunt Sophie is."

"Look, Alicia," I said, partly to keep the talk away from me, and partly because it seemed to me she needed some good advice. "I don't think the girls treat you like that because you're so smart. It's just that

76

you're always *talking* about being so smart and *acting* like you think you're so smart. I mean . . ." She narrowed her eyes at me, and I was sorry I'd said it. I didn't know for sure what I'd said wrong, though. I mean, it was true. I wasn't lying or anything.

She stuck her chin out. "What are you suggesting?" she asked, cold as ice.

"Well, I mean, like telling everybody what grades you get on your tests and sort of expecting people to tell you what they got when you know they didn't do as good as you. And stuff like yesterday telling those girls who sit behind me how your parents think you ought to skip a grade or maybe it was two grades. I don't know. I mean . . ." and I started digging around in the bag again, without looking at her. "Stuff like that makes people think *you* think you're better than they are."

"Maybe I am," she said.

"Maybe." I shrugged. Maybe she was, for all I knew. "But I don't think people like people much who are different."

"Are you different?" she asked me. She sounded almost kind. Or maybe she was pretending to be a psychiatrist.

"I don't know," I told her.

"OK, then, if *you're* so smart, what should I talk to them about?"

"How do I know? I think they talk a lot about boys—and whatever kind of stuff girls do after school. I don't know."

"Well, I don't know what they do after school because they don't ask me to do it with them." She stared at me like it was my fault. "You want me to talk about *you?*"

"Geez, no. Look, forget I said it." I turned my back to her. My face got as hot as if somebody had plugged it in. Sometimes I talk too much.

"Sammy," Alicia said, like Mrs. Bird does, "you really couldn't read that report title, could you?"

"Me? Oh, sure," I lied. "I was just making a little joke there. Fresh-French. Very funny, no?"

"No," Alicia answered. "I looked closely at the Viking test you passed up to me yesterday, and some of your spelling . . ."

I didn't say anything. There wasn't anything for Old Retard to say. Besides, it wasn't any of her business. So we kept searching, without saying anything and without finding much—some pennies, a plastic orange barrette, and a yellow coin purse with a smiley face on it.

Wally burst into the garbage room, still trying to hold his breath and talk at the same time. "She says OK, but hurry up or we'll miss all the Social Studies movie."

Then, just as he grabbed his nose and tried to open

his bag again, I found the retainer, mashed over to the side of my bag. And here I'd been all the time plowing through the middle.

"Found it!" I yelled, digging it out and flipping it over to him in a high pop-up. "At least it's somebody's retainer, though for all I know it's some fourth-grade girl's."

His face fell. "Do you think so?" he asked. But when I grinned he shook his head and looked at it close. "Can't be two lost or we'd have had some help in here."

"What do you mean, 'we'?" Alicia called after him as he waved the retainer in the air and disappeared, yelling, "I'll wash it off and try it on!"

While I tied up the garbage bags, Alicia gathered up the money, the yellow purse, the report, and some other junk from the floor. I fled from the green room and Alicia ran after me.

The class was already looking at this movie on the crossing of the Mayflower. When we walked in, the huge mast was cracking below deck and all the Pilgrims were panicking because they thought they were all going under. For school movies it wasn't half bad.

Mrs. Bird nodded to us.

"Where do you suppose Priss Bliss and the new kid have been?" the girl behind me asked somebody.

Wally came in just after we did, smiling, the retainer snug in his mouth. As he sat down, Alicia said, loud enough for the girl in back of me to hear, "*We just found Wally's retainer in the lunch trash.*"

Wally groaned. "Geez, Alicia." The class broke up laughing just as some sailor in the movie was shouting, "Land Ho!" A couple of girls leaned over in the dark and giggled with Alicia.

"Were you with Wally and the new kid all that time?" one of them asked her. She smiled and tossed her hair.

"All alone in a very small room," she told them. "Wally's shy, but Sammy's cute," she said.

The girl behind me leaned forward. "Have a good time?" she asked, poking me in the shoulder. I could have died.

The movie was over just at three and when the bell rang I dashed out the door before anybody else got their eyes adjusted to the light. I had to escape from both Bird and Bliss.

As I ran I patted my jeans pocket to check that my tornado story was there, but the pocket was flat. I stopped a minute to dig around inside, but there wasn't any paper to find. I'd lost it. A half hour's work and I'd lost it.

"Sammy Mott!" I heard Mrs. Bird shout and I darted away to meet the boys.

"Oh, Sam-my," Alicia called.

I escaped, but with the Bird chirping down my back. And Priss Bliss right behind her.

5

VIKING STUFF

ALEX STOOD THERE like a normal kid waiting at the kindergarten door. Spiderman crouched on the windowsill, ready to leap.

"*Aieeeee!*" he yelled, and threw himself straight at my neck. I cleverly stepped to the side like a proper supervillain would and Spidey fell flat on the dandelions. He was up in a minute.

"The Magnet Men are after us," I told them. "Run like crazy or they'll yank us back in school." So we ran like crazy all the way to their house. All the time I tried to remember putting the twister paper somewhere else. Sometimes I forget where I put stuff, but this time my pocket was the only place it could have been. I *knew* I hadn't left it in my desk. Oh, well, I thought, who cares?

"Today," I said, as the boys started stuffing bananas into their mouths, "today we're going to the jungle. And we'll climb a jungle tree—ta daaah—starting at the top."

"Don't you mean the 'pot'?" Alex asked, grinning at me.

I bopped him on the head. "That was just a *joke*," I said, bopping him again, harder.

"Don't hit my brother," Chuck shouted, slugging me.

"You told us it was a *mistake*," Alex said, punching me harder than I'd bopped him. "My mom said that was a funny mistake—funny strange not funny ha-ha."

"You *told* her?"

"Sure, why not?" Alex asked.

Why did they have to go and do that? She wouldn't need to be Sherlock Holmes to figure out all those clues. Pretty soon, I thought, they're all going to know and I'll be Dumbhead Sam again. Being stupid is like having a birthmark. You can hide it, but you've still got it. I ate three bananas.

"We're gonna climb our tree, aren't we?" Chuck asked, shaking my shoulder. "Before they come and saw it up and take it away?"

I didn't answer him. I just banged out of the kitchen and let the screen door slam.

The backyard was filled with tree. Its branches reached all the way to the neighbor's fence and there were huge hills of leaves. The trunk had been pulled clear out of the ground. It made you feel sad like a big dog had died or some wild thing, like a raccoon or a squirrel, had been hit by a car.

We started at the top (pot) where Chuck found an empty bird's nest, empty except for some blue-green eggshells caught in the twigs. He dug around underneath as far as he could for baby birds, but we decided they'd flown away weeks ago. Two squirrels playing tag in the lower branches ran away when they saw us coming.

Chuck hopped down the branches like a lumberjack riding logs on a river. "Hey, you guys," he yelled. "You're not gonna believe this. I found a truck."

"A truck? That was some tornado." I started crawling through the brush to take a look. A Jeep? I wondered. A branch flew back and hit me in the face.

It *was* a truck. Chuck was holding it up. A toy yellow earth mover, its scoop filled with a cupful of dirt. "I bet that tornado sucked it over. It was in the garden last week. That's cool," Chuck sighed.

The tree had pulled up a whole batch of dirt, and now that the rain had stopped, the earth was fine and soft, clinging to all the tiny roots. They were just beginning to droop. The trunk was so big I couldn't reach around it. It must have been very old. It wasn't fair it should fall and die.

Chuck slithered into the hole where the roots had been, tearing a path with his sneakers. It was almost three feet deep.

"It's a spooky cave," Alex said, pushing his way down, too.

"There are black bugs down here," Chuck called. "This one's friendly. Look."

I lay down on the trunk of the tree and reached into the finest of the roots. They looked soft like moss. I knew tree roots were supposed to drink in water. I wondered if they were wet.

The ones on top were dry, so I stuck my hand farther into the middle. I didn't strike water. I struck metal.

"Hey, I found something," I called, and the boys scrambled through the hairy brush. "It's stuck."

"Another truck?" Chuck asked.

I pulled, but whatever it was had roots twined all around it. Settling my feet as well as I could, I gave one swift yank. It pulled free, and I went rolling off onto the ground. I just lay there, looking at what I had found. It was all rusty and full of pits, but it was something, at least it *used* to be something. It was about a foot long and shaped like a small shovel. There was a lot of dirt inside the handle.

I didn't know what it was, but I knew for sure it didn't blow in from the garden. It had been knotted up deep in those roots for a long time.

"It's just a broken-off piece of something," Alex said, turning it over in his hand.

"Maybe some Viking left it," Chuck said.

"Maybe," I told him. I mean, why not? Those Vikings sailed just about everywhere else. Why not

Lake Michigan? "Maybe it's a Viking tool of some kind," I said, just to keep him going. "Let's see if there's more."

"A sword," Chuck yelled. "I want a sword they chopped people up with."

We started tearing off roots and digging like madmen. The dirt smelled clean. Not like the garbage did at noon. It had that good smell, like after a hard rain.

"I'll go get a shovel from the basement," Alex said. "I bet there'll be dinosaur bones, too. And he flashed across the backyard like a kid in an ad for Keds.

Chuck and me started digging with our hands, lifting out dirt and pushing root branches aside.

"Are you running away to China?" a voice above us asked.

I looked up and groaned. "Alicia," I said. She smiled sweetly like nothing had happened. "That was some stupid thing to say in class," I told her. "Thanks a whole lot."

"This is our yard and we found something in it," Chuck said. "Who are you?"

"Alicia," she told him. "I'm Sam's friend." She grinned like she'd just won a big chess game or something. "Oh, I don't know," she said to me. "I expect it wasn't stupid at all. I was just taking your advice. And it worked. They started talking to me after school."

"How did you know I was here?" I asked her.

"Wally told me," she said. "But you know, he really *is* shy."

I wasn't exactly crazy about Alicia coming up and saying she was my friend and all, but nobody was looking and how often do you find treasure under a tree, anyway? "Look, it's got to be ages old," I bragged. And I held the rusty pipe thing up for her to see.

She took it, turned it around in her hands a few times, and shrugged her shoulders. "It doesn't look like much." Then she leaned over and looked closer at the hole. "Can I help? I'm practically a professional digger. I found a silver treasure today." She sat down on the grass and showed Chuck the handful of coins.

"We don't even know what we're looking for," I told her. She sat there, smug, like she knew a secret.

"I found something of yours," she said finally, taking a piece of paper from her purse and flapping it at me. It was the old creative twister paper.

I grabbed it, stuffed it in my pocket, and said, "It's just doodling. It's nothing." But by the way she smiled I knew she'd read it over and figured out I was Dumbhead Sam.

Alex arrived with the shovel. At first Chuck and Alex took turns fighting over who was to dig. I turned away from Alicia and watched them unearth a few night crawlers. When the ground got harder, they decided to turn the shovel over to me. The hole was crowded. Alex and Chuck wanted to stay down where

86

the action was, but that made it hard to move the shovel. Roots and kids and me—that was a lot for one hole. I kept whopping one of them with the handle or raining dirt down their necks. Alicia ordered them out, but they stayed put. She didn't say anything to me.

"Maybe we'll find gold," Alex said.

"Or oil," I told him, feeling better just thinking about finding something.

"Or just more roots," Alicia said, matter-of-fact.

Clink, the shovel hit something.

"Watch out, you'll break it," Chuck yelled. "I bet it's the sword." It didn't sound like metal, but it didn't sound like a root either. We all three clawed around it with our fingernails. Chuck pulled it out. It was just a rock covered with dirt.

"Alex, get some water, fast. We'll wash it," I said to get him out of the hole, and he sprinted off again. While he was gone we dug up a smooth stone, about fist size, with one end cracked off.

"It's another dinosaur egg," I yelled, and Chuck threw a fistful of dirt at me.

Every spade I turned had something in it. Pretty soon we had a whole pile of rocks and junk. When Alex came with the water we stuck everything inside, put our hands in, and tried to swoosh it around and scrub the dirt off. The muddy water spilled over onto Alex's already gray sneakers.

Alicia pulled the first thing out of the pail. And for

the first time she got excited. "I think it's part of a pot," she said. "See how smooth it is?"

"You mean a 'top,' don't you?" Alex asked, giggling and giving me a poke in the ribs. He was going to beat that joke to death, and bash a hole in my side while he did it.

Alicia gave me a questioning look, and I shoved Alex over into the tree branches.

"Who tracked mud in my kitchen?" Mrs. Glass was standing behind us. (Did she see me shove her kid?) She said it like she was saying hello, not like she wanted to know who tracked mud in her kitchen. I guess she was used to mud. "What are you doing? Maybe I should have them leave this tree out here a few weeks instead of cutting it up tomorrow. It's better than a jungle gym. Alex, your shoes are disgusting."

"I'm Alicia Bliss," Alicia said, holding out her hand. But it was muddy wet, so she and Mrs. Glass both just looked at it. "I'm Sam's very good friend."

"Oh, Sam, you've got a girl friend," Mrs. Glass said, snickering like she was in sixth grade.

Alex and Chuck started showing her the stuff we'd found.

"Hey," she said, "this looks great. I love the little metal scoop. And that *does* look like part of an old pot." She kind of bounced up and down. "I'll tell you what. We'll call the paper. Maybe they'll come over and take our picture. Or maybe, anyway, somebody there can tell us where we can find out what this stuff is."

"It's Viking stuff," Chuck told her. "Sam said."

"Fancy that. I love it. I absolutely love it. Sam, you run in and call the paper, will you?" Then her face fell. "Oh, I forgot, you can't . . ." Alicia looked startled, like she was surprised somebody else knew, too.

Mrs. G. started in toward the house. "Look, you kids stay out of my kitchen, will you? Burrow around under the roots some more. You keep the dirt outside and I'll call the editor of the *News Advertiser* right now. I *met* him yesterday," she called over her shoulder.

We didn't find much while she was gone—some chips of rock we saved in the bucket. They didn't look like anything, but we sure found a bunch of them.

"Listen," Mrs. Glass called as she ran toward us, pushing the hair out of her eyes. "I've been on the phone *all* this time. Everybody said I should talk to somebody else. What a hassle. The editor wasn't too hot about sending somebody out to take a picture. He said he had a million storm pictures already, so I brought the Polaroid out. Flop over in the branches and smile."

We smiled and then watched the picture develop into leaf-green and dirty brown. We looked like mud-caked soldiers camouflaged to hide in the sideways tree behind us.

"Anyway," she went on, "he said for me to call the Historical Society, which was a pretty smart idea, but of course nobody was there this late. So I called the Randall University number and they transferred me to the archeology department and there was this one woman still there. So I told her we had found some Viking artifacts under an ancient tree in our backyard."

"*Viking?*" Alicia yelped. "You're kidding."

"You really told her *that?*" I moaned. "I doubt it's really Viking stuff."

"Oh, me, too," Mrs. Glass sighed, "but who's going to come and look if I say it's a bunch of broken stones and an old rusty pipe? Besides, Chuckie said that's what you said." She smiled at me, showing her crooked teeth. "I don't think this archeologist person believed it was Viking artifacts, either, but she did say she'd stop by on her way home. We don't have anything to lose. Sam, take my picture with the tree," she said, handing me the camera.

"Did you find anything else good?" she asked as I took the picture.

"You moved your mouth," Chuck said.

"Oh, well, then, take another." She smiled without showing her teeth for the picture.

"I've got to leave now," Alicia said. Then she lowered her voice. "Mrs. Bird was looking for you after school," she whispered to me. "She was mad you didn't wait."

"Come on, kids. Sam wants to talk to his girl," Mrs. Glass said to them, laughing.

"I just thought you ought to know," Alicia went on, "Mrs. Bird is going to call your parents about you. I heard her tell Miss Meredith, and I thought I should warn you." She looked at me hard to see how I was taking it, so I didn't flinch.

"They're not home," I told her.

She sighed, like she was terribly, terribly worried about me. "That's something, I guess. Now, Sammy, if you ever want to know how to spell anything or read anything—even the simplest little words—I'll be glad to help. I'm so sorry," she cooed, like I was a three-year-old. I could have smacked her one, like I was a three-year-old.

"Look, just buzz off," I said, mad. "I don't need any help from you or anybody else." She stood there looking for a minute like I *had* smacked her one. "And you sure don't need to feel sorry for me," I went on. "I can take care of myself."

"Oh," she said, and then smiled brightly. "You're upset because I know you can't spell, aren't you? Don't worry, I won't tell. I think you're cute." She turned and skipped out the driveway.

YOU DIG?

THE GLASSES were grubbing away, tossing things into the bucket of water and laughing like crazy. "Why don't you help us dig?" Mrs. Glass asked me. "Unless you have to go home. It must be almost five-thirty." I wanted to dig. I would have if I'd been by myself, but I thought if I joined those three, Alex and Chuck would probably start the stupid top-pot stuff again.

Nobody was home at my house so I just lay down on the grass and shuffled through a patch of dark green clover, trying to find one with four lucky leaves. I needed it. I really needed it. But my finding power had left me. I rested my chin on the ground and searched for leprechauns under the clover. If I found one and it gave me a wish, I said to myself, I wouldn't be greedy like those guys in stories who ask for marble castles or chests of gold or power over the sun and the moon and the universe. All I'd ask for would be to read and write as good as Wally Whiteside. Not even to be a big brain like Alicia Bliss. Just one little easy wish.

"Sam, what are you thinking about over there?" Mrs. Glass called.

I picked up a maple seed, split open the sticky end, fastened it on my nose, and sat up. It arched up just right. "I'm a rhinoceros," I said, "thinking rhinoceros thoughts."

"You're crazy," Chuck called, laughing. "Sam's crazy," he told his mother.

"We're finding dinosaur bones," Alex said. "Come see."

"Dog bones, more likely." His mother waved something at me.

I plucked the rhino horn off my nose and walked over.

"Is this Viking Village?" a voice called out. Down the driveway on a sun-yellow moped tooled this girl who was probably in college. I mean, about that old. Not much older, anyway. She wore a pack on her back and jeans with knees that had worn through to the very last threads. Her long brown hair was pulled back in a ponytail and on her T-shirt was printed YOU DIG? I could read it. It was a cool T-shirt.

"Brenda Strawhacker," she said, hopping off the moped and shedding her pack, "archeologist, third class." She stuck out her hand for somebody to shake. Chuck grabbed it with a muddy paw.

"I'm Chuck," he said. "I found the truck."

She didn't even blink. "Mostly," she said to him

93

very seriously, "Vikings went in for dragon ships and sleds and wagons—some of them elaborately carved. But you hardly ever—even in Illinois—find Viking trucks."

"Uh, hi," Mrs. Glass mumbled, scrambling out of the tree hole. "I'm Marietta Glass. This is Alex. He's also mine. And that's Sam. He's a friend." She was a total mess. She hadn't even changed since she'd gotten home from work except to take off her shoes. Her pink striped skirt looked like it was never going to be clean again, not even with New Formula Tide.

Chuck grabbed his yellow dump truck and gave it to Brenda, who looked pleased.

"It's mine," he told her. "The tornado whipped it into the hole."

"Sam says some Viking guy left this, though," Alex told her, reaching for my little metal spade.

"I didn't—I never said that. I just—just said *maybe*, that's all," I stammered out, grabbing the rusty thing from him. "It's probably nothing. But it was way down in the roots of the tree."

Brenda took it from me, narrowing her eyes as she inspected it, scraping at the rust with her fingernail. "What do you think?" she asked me.

I shrugged my shoulders. I wasn't going to say anything else dumb.

"Do you know what it is?" Mrs. Glass asked her.

"Um . . . I can guess," Brenda said, and she started cleaning mud out of the handle with a twig.

"So can I," Chuck said. "It's a kid's beach shovel."

"Looks like it, doesn't it? Look at that. The handle's a hollow tube. That's a clue, all right." She sat on her heels in the grass, and it looked like the right thing to do so we sat, too, in a little circle around the water pail. "Caught in the roots of a tree that big, it's got to be at least a hundred years old. I don't think they had nineteenth-century beach toys."

"Only a hundred?" Alex said. I guess he was really counting on the Vikings. Or maybe a dinosaur.

"Come on, you're lucky the iron lasted this long." She flicked off a piece of rust and started to tell us this story about what we'd found. No kidding, she looked at this crummy crusty piece of pipe and started telling us about how farmers used to live right where we were sitting. She said how there were forests of sugar maple trees and how they drilled holes in the trees and stuck in these pipes so the maple sap could drip out. She called the pipe I found a tapping gouge, and said the sweet sap used to drip out of it in the spring and the farmers would gather the sap in buckets and heat it to make maple syrup.

I looked at that rusty pipe and I could hardly believe some farmer a hundred years ago had left it outside, dropping it by mistake or something. Or maybe, I thought, it was his dumb kid who'd lost it. That farmer probably got mad at his kid and sent him back out to look, but the kid still couldn't find it. And then one of those maple seeds like I'd had on my nose dropped on the ground next to it and a tree grew all around it, right there.

I wondered if the kid who'd lost the tapping gouge could read and spell. Maybe you didn't have to back then.

"That was some stroke of luck," Brenda said. "Lots of things like that are never found, though I'm not sure losing this huge maple tree was worth it." We all looked over at the big tree that had become a kind of friend by now, sharing its secret with us.

"Is it fun, being an archeologist?" I asked her.

"Sure," she said. "And work. I'm going next week to our big dig in southern Illinois."

That's what I'd like to be, I decided. That's what I'd really like to be, an archeologist. To dig and find good stuff and tell people about how it got there. I mean, not just finding junk and piling it up in orange crates, but really *knowing* about it.

"Well," Alex said, turning the gouge over in his hand, "it's not gold and the Vikings didn't leave it, but it's not bad."

"Got anything else?" Brenda asked.

Mrs. Glass stirred the stuff in the bucket with her

hand. "They found a whole bucket of things—just junk probably—gravel and filler. You don't want to bother with it. It's all dirty." She stood up. "Thanks for coming, though. No kidding. We appreciate it."

"Come on," Brenda said, "don't hold out on me. What have you got?"

Chuck tried to lift the bucket, but it was too heavy, so he tipped the whole mess over onto the grass. We were all pretty embarrassed by it—a landslide of muddy rocks. Brenda picked up several pieces and rubbed them between her fingers. "Where'd you find these?"

"Hiding under the big old treasure tree," Mrs. G. said, clearly tired of the whole thing. She grabbed the camera and took a picture of Brenda, the boys, and the mud pile.

"No kidding? This is really great," Brenda said as she sifted through the mud. "In the dirt *under* the gouge? Look, I'd probably have to know more than I do now, but I'd swear this is from a garbage pit."

"Good grief," Mrs. G. moaned, rubbing her hands on her skirt.

"Garbage?" Alex asked, staring into the rubble.

"Right. It's excellent," she said, obviously excited about something the rest of us missed.

"Excellent?" Chuck asked her.

"What's so excellent about garbage?" I asked.

"Oh," she said, catching on that we didn't know

why she was pleased. "Listen, I'm not putting it down by calling it garbage. You can learn a lot about people from what they throw away."

I thought about how I'd pawed through all those french fries and unopened peanut butter and jelly sandwiches and how we'd even found money thrown away at school. I wondered what an archeologist would make of that.

"Alex," Mrs. Glass said, "go fill the bucket with some clean water. I want to wash my hands." She started cleaning the mud off her pink polished toenails. "What's garbage about this bunch of rocks?" she asked.

"Well," Brenda said, sitting cross-legged like she was going to tell us a long story, "it looks like the kind of leftover, broken things that Indians threw away, perhaps before the settlers moved in. The Potawatomies used to live around here."

"What's Potawatomi?" Chuck asked.

"An Indian," I told him. "Potawatomi was his tribe." I knew that from television. "Potawatomi and Iroquois and Apache and other guys like that."

"Right. Well, anyway," Brenda went on, "the Potawatomies had their winter quarters here at the tip of Lake Michigan. When they didn't need something anymore, they threw it in a hole they'd made for garbage." She picked up the piece Alicia had said looked like a pot.

"This," she said, "is a broken piece of pottery. They

must have tossed it in the garbage pit because it was broken. Here," and she shoved a few pieces aside to leave one by itself. "This is a broken flint—a chip left over from making points. There are lots of them in your pile."

"Like arrowheads?" Alex asked, setting down the bucket of water. "A kid in my class brought arrowheads for Show and Tell."

"Sure, arrowheads and scrapers and knives and spearheads. They're all points."

"Somebody sitting in our backyard making arrowheads," Mrs. G. said, washing her hands in the bucket. "Fancy that, Chuckie, an Indian sitting under our maple tree."

"Mother," Alex sighed. "The maple tree grew on *top* of the Indian stuff. The garbage was here before the tree was."

"Is this a dinosaur bone, at least?" Chuck asked, holding up the biggest piece of garbage.

"Nope. Probably deer."

"But when?" I asked her. "When was all this?"

"Got me," Brenda said. "I can't read it."

"What do you mean, *read* it? Nobody can read rocks and bones."

"Oh, sure they can. Somebody who knows a whole lot more than I do can tell you for sure what Indians made that pot just from looking at the pieces, and they might even be able to tell you what the pot was used for. And they could solve the mystery of the bones. If you know what you're doing you can read the dirt, too, and even tell how long people lived here."

Chuck slid down into the hole. "I've lived here five years," he said, "and I found this hole first."

"What *I'm* going to do," Alex said, picking up the shovel, "is to dig up the rest of the yard. Maybe I'll find a skeleton."

"Yeah, a skeleton," Chuck yelled from the hole. He jumped out and yanked the shovel away from Alex, who howled.

"Oh, cut it out," Brenda called. "Look, friends, the only reason you found this stuff is that the tree was over it. The rest of your yard has been plowed and planted and dug up for years. Nothing's there anymore. The tree saved this one small pocket of treasure for you."

"Poor tree," Mrs. Glass said. She grabbed the shovel from the boys and started off for the house with it.

Chuck and Alex burrowed under the branches.

"You have to read a lot to be an archeologist?" I asked Brenda. "Books, I mean, not dirt and bones. Do you have to be smart?"

"I don't know. You want to see one of my books?" She reached in her pack and pulled out one that had a skeleton on the cover. It was a big book, bigger than anything I was sure I could ever read. Even after she told me what the title was, it took me awhile to read all the words.

So finding stuff wasn't enough. Knowing a few Indian names from TV sure wasn't enough. You had to be able to read the rocks and the dirt and you couldn't do that unless you could read books harder than second grade. And I couldn't. Imagine Sam Mott, big deal archeologist, bringing his father along to read to him every night.

I looked up and saw Brenda staring at me, puzzled. I guess I was crying or something. So I just got up and left her there. I walked down the driveway as fast as I could. It wasn't fair. All those things I wanted to do. It just wasn't fair.

7
A LITTLE TALK ABOUT SAMMY

THE WARM SMELL of morning coffee drifted into the bathroom and I could hear Mom and Dad in the kitchen arguing. About me. It had to be about me. They wouldn't have anything else to argue about. If they got a divorce because of me, I wondered which one I would live with.

"Breakfast! Get your hot breakfast here!" Mom called. I finished brushing my bracey teeth, rinsed my mouth out, and smiled into the mirror. My face still had smudges of maple tree dirt on it from last night. I rubbed at them with a towel.

"*Now*, Samuel!" she called. "It's getting late."

Tossing the towel into the bathtub, I glanced at the sink. It was ringed with dirt and the blue toothpaste had wormed out of its tube. The cap was on the floor. Mom would hate all that. But she'd said "now." So I pushed down on my hair and hurried, shoeless, into the kitchen.

Dad was reading the paper. "You'll be certain to

apologize to Mrs. Bird about yesterday," he said, without looking up. I'd already promised him the night before I would. Why did he have to start off like that?

"Good morning," I said, and he looked up and smiled. Everybody says I look just like him. I can't see it much, but it's true his hair and eyebrows are bushy like mine. He can separate his toes like I can, too. Except now he had on shoes. Loafers. I wish they'd let me wear loafers. You don't have to tie them so they aren't all the time coming untied. And he was wearing this suit with a vest.

"Do we bug you, Sam?" he asked.

I shrugged my shoulders. "I don't know," I said and sat down in front of my powdered sugar doughnut.

"Nonsense," my mom told him. "It's our duty to see he's disciplined." She shook her head and her hair sort of scooted from side to side. When it finally fell still, it looked like a small brown cap. She was wearing a suit, too, only hers didn't have a vest. They both looked important, like they gave orders and people did what they said to do. "Ernie, he's got to understand that what he did was wrong." She turned to me. "Right?"

I was looking at the pearls she was wearing. They were just like the ones I'd dreamed of finding on the beach. Shiny white pearls. "Right?" I heard her ask me again.

"I guess," I answered.

" 'I guess' doesn't cut it, Sam. Explain to me," she said, "why you didn't just tell Mrs. Bird you had to baby-sit instead of running away like that." She cracked the breakfast eggs into a blue and white bowl and went at them with a fork like she'd show them a thing or two.

"I didn't have time," I told her. "I was already late for Chuck and Alex and I didn't want them to leave without me." That wasn't the pure truth. I wasn't late, but it sounded like I'd been very trustworthy. "Besides," I barked at them, "it couldn't have been all that important that she had to call Dad up last night and yell about me."

"Oh, cut it out," Dad said mildly, pouring us all some coffee. "She was actually very nice. All she said was that she wanted to have a little talk about Sammy."

"Do I look like a Sammy?" I asked him. "No kidding, do I *look* like a Sammy?" I dunked my doughnut in the coffee and watched the powdered sugar melt. I always get coffee when we have doughnuts. Ever since I was little I've liked the way it tastes and the way it makes the doughnut warm and crumbly so it just melts in your mouth. I stirred it around and took a bite. It was delicious.

Dad glanced at Mom with a worried look that scared me. She rolled her eyes up at him, dashed the scrambled eggs onto our plates, and sat down.

"Sam," she said, "sit up and eat your breakfast."

I picked up the pepper grinder and started grinding.

"Well," she went on, "Mrs. Bird told your father the reason she wanted you to stay after school yesterday was so she could tell you about the testing program that's been arranged for you."

"Testing?" I asked. Although I'd heard them talking about it a few mornings ago, I'd hoped it would go away by itself. I didn't remember hearing Dad say anything about testing when he was on the phone last night. The Bird did most of the talking, though, and mostly I remember Dad saying, "Well, no," and "I see," and "He must have had a very good reason," and "We feel he's adjusting very well to the new school environment," and "I'm sure everything is going to be all right," and "Oh, fine, oh, fine," "Splendid," "Fine," "We'll tell him then. . . ." Of course, *that* was it. "*We'll* tell him then." And they were telling me. Well, I'd tell them, too.

"You remember, Sam, like the tests in California. They were kind of fun, weren't they? Like games?" Mom stared down at her plate and pushed the eggs around on it with her fork.

"Why should I do that all over again? Couldn't they just send for last year's tests? That'll tell them how dumb I am. That's what tests are for, aren't they?"

"Enough of that, Sam," Dad said. "Look, your mother and I thought that if you started out with a whole new battery of tests, different from those in California, they'd find something new. You're a year older now and a year smarter."

I stared at him like he wasn't putting anything over on *me*. He'd heard me read and read to me. He'd written stuff for me, guiding my hand. Since I was a little kid. He looked down at his eggs and half-eaten doughnut. I knew he wouldn't be able to look me in the eye.

"Mrs. Bird said," Mom went on, taking over for him, "we should tell you that these tests will tell her how it is easiest for you to learn. That's simple enough."

"Well, I won't do it. They'll just ask me all kinds of stuff I don't know. I won't do it."

"You'll do it. Your mother signed the permission slip last week," Dad said. He pulled out the sports section of the newspaper and started to look at the baseball scores.

"Sam?" Mom asked, scooting her chair round to mine at the table. "Look, can you read this?" She leafed through the paper to the comics and pointed at a balloon of words over somebody's head.

I took a deep breath. "Do I have to?"

"Come on," she said, pointing and squinting at the print as though she was figuring out how hard it was going to be.

I narrowed my eyes, too, and *knew*. There were some long words and those were always killers.

"Good . . ." I read, and that was right. I knew it

was. I looked up at her to say hooray, but she just kept pointing. "Good . . . after . . . noon . . . Lie . . . Lie . . . Lie . . ."

"Lieutenant," she said. "That's a hard one, granted. 'Good afternoon, Lieutenant.' " And she kept her finger on the spot. "From here on it's as easy as instant breakfast. Sam, sit up. You'll grow a hump the size of a watermelon."

"This is stupid," I groaned, shutting the newspaper on top of her hand. "What's this got to do with tests?" This was an old thing with us, a routine we'd set up a long time ago. Mom would say, "Read this, it's really easy," and then I'd try and fail and usually she'd shout at me. I'd end up feeling like a rotten onion.

She gave me her no-nonsense look. "I just wanted to show you why you have to take the tests. You can only read the easy words. And you don't read those well enough. Somehow the schools haven't taught you to read properly, and we're going to find out why."

My dad took a deep breath. "Mrs. Bird said to tell you there'll be two tests, once this Monday and another the next Monday, and altogether they'll take about seven hours."

"*Seven hours!* Geez! That's a marathon! Everybody'll say, 'There goes old Dumbhead Sam, taking the dumbhead tests.' Forget it." I cocked my head, stuck my tongue out the side of my mouth, and gave them my idiot kid look.

"Forget your 'forget it,'" Mom said, rinsing off her plate and putting it in the dishwasher. "And I'm going to be late for the train if I don't blast out of here pretty soon."

I scraped my uneaten eggs into the garbage disposal, put my plate in the dishwasher, and said, "Seven hours! They can't make me do it."

"Sam," she said, rubbing my neck like she does sometimes, "I love you dearly. Notwithstanding the mess in your room and your crazy reading, you are a joy and a delight. I just want you to be able to read and write as well as any other kid. I don't want you to go down the drain."

I turned on the water and started the garbage disposal. (*Glub, glub, glub,* I was halfway down the drain already.)

"We're going to get your eyes tested again," Dad said weakly, like he thought I'd complain about that, too. They'd never found anything wrong with my eyes before. I didn't see how they'd start now.

Mom pushed the button on her digital watch. "Gotta run," she said. "Seven-forty." She grabbed her briefcase and hurried out the kitchen door.

Dad gulped down some more coffee and followed after to catch the 7:55. The screen door slammed after him and I watched him kick a chimney brick out into the street. "Don't forget your homework," he called back.

"I don't have any," I snapped, and hunched over the sink. I didn't have the storm paper because I'd torn it up into very, very, very small pieces and flushed it. I hadn't asked Dad to help me with a new one last night, either. I'd watched TV instead. A movie about two crazy old ladies who were killers. It was pretty funny.

Leaving the rest of the dishes on the table, I went into my folks' bedroom and turned on the color TV. There was a black and white Tarzan movie on.

"Jane say Boy sick?" Tarzan asked her. He put his hand on Boy's forehead. "Boy has bubonic plague. Tarzan cure." And he did. I love old movies.

At eight-thirty I had to turn it off without knowing if Tarzan broke his neck when the vine got shot through and he fell into the deep ravine. I had to get to school early to say I was sorry. I'd promised.

LOSERS WEEPERS

ON PURPOSE I was the first one in the room. I didn't want anybody hanging around that conversation. Mrs. Bird peered at me over her little half-moon glasses. "Well?" she asked.

So like a good boy I told her what a bad boy I was. You know. I told her how I'd just remembered at three o'clock about my baby-sitting job and the little tiny kids waiting for me and how scared they would have been if I was late and how they might have run out in the street and gotten smashed by a speeding car. She got tired of listening and waved her hand back and forth to make me stop.

"Next time, Sammy, make your explanations ahead of time." She shoved a few papers around on her desk and then looked up at me again. "Did your parents explain to you about the tests on Monday, Sammy?" People were starting to drift into the room.

"Um," I said, shrugging.

"Don't you worry about them for a minute," she

oozed like maple syrup. "Everything's going to be fine."

Worry? Worry? Why should I worry about two days of gruesome questions? Could Mom sign my life away like that? Could she? I was sure if I did take them, they'd be worse than the ones in California where the man kept making me try to spell words I *knew* I didn't know how to spell. I got cramps in my stomach then and the guy giving the test didn't smile or frown. He just sat there firing words at me with his face looking like a piece of gray cardboard. I already knew that if I *did* take those tests (which I wasn't going to), they'd say I belonged back in fifth grade. Or maybe even in second with Alex. And wouldn't that be a riot.

I wandered around the room, waiting for the bell to ring, kicking desks out of their lines. On the bulletin board there was a terrific newspaper picture of the two funnel clouds. Four twister stories were already tacked up. Alicia's was one of them. I could tell by the neat handwriting. It figured. Mine wasn't. It was down the john.

"Careful," a kid called out, and a couple of girls came backing into the room, helping Alicia carry her huge science project. It was something about solar energy that you had to read a thousand books about before you could do it. I didn't even know what to *do* mine on.

"Oh, hi, Sammy," Alicia called sweetly.

"Hi, Sammy," one of the other girls said. "Alicia told us you and her were digging up somebody's backyard yesterday looking for Vikings." She laughed mysteriously, like that was supposed to be some big secret.

"She told us a lot about you-ou," the other one sang out. Alicia had already told them I was a dumbhead. Didn't waste any time. I guess I knew she wouldn't keep it a secret.

They all laughed. It was an inside joke. My insides.

Wally came in, flicking a yo-yo in front of him.

The girls laughed, but it didn't sound like the same kind of laugh.

He let me use the yo-yo and I walked the dog with it and did around-the-world, but the girls had already gone away.

"Sam," he said to me, "no kidding, I'm sorry I told Alicia where you were after school yesterday. Did she find you?"

I rolled my eyes to let him know she sure did.

"I hope she didn't bug you too much. But she was following me home. She said if I didn't tell her where you were she'd tell my mother about my tossing the retainer in the trash. Can you *believe* that?"

"That's blackmail," I said. "This guy on the late show the other night told a lady who had these pictures of him, 'I won't pay you ten grand because that's blackmail pure and simple!'"

"Yeah, well, I paid. Or, anyway, you did. I'm sorry."

He tried to walk the dog with his yo-yo, but it just hung there at the end of the string. "Dead dog," he said and rolled it up. "Hey, look, you want to come over tomorrow? My mom's taking me and my sister fossil hunting in Coal City, and she said we could each ask somebody. We take hammers and everything for busting open the rocks. It's really cool."

"Would I ever!" I told him, feeling much better. "My folks took me once to this place hunting for Herkimer diamonds—they're just quartz, really, but they sparkle like diamonds, so that's what they call them. Anyway, I found three big ones. Everybody was coming around looking at them and all. It was neat."

"Come at eight-thirty. It's a couple hours' drive."

"Where do you live?"

"Over on Forest. I'll write it down for you. What did Alicia want you so bad for yesterday anyway?"

"She . . . she's . . ." I started, but I couldn't tell him what Alicia knew about me. And what the other girls probably knew. And Mrs. Bird. And then I just blinked and knew that Wally wasn't going to be my real friend either. Not when he found out. Who wants a dope for a friend? "Oh," I told him, "she just wanted to tell me Mrs. Bird was looking for me after school."

"Yeah, she was. I heard her shouting after you down the hall. But you were sailing out of here like an electric Frisbee."

The last bell rang and everybody shuffled around to

their seats. After attendance, cafeteria count, and current events, Mrs. Bird announced, "People, today is Friday the thirteenth. And to dispel the superstition that this is an unlucky day, I thought we might do something special, just for fun. Instead of the spelling test scheduled for this morning—which *might* have been unlucky for some of you—we'll have . . ." and she paused and laughed a little at how clever she was. (A morning of recess? I wondered. Cartoons and pizza? No more school ever?) "A spelling bee, an old-fashioned spelling bee," she said.

Nobody whooped for sheer joy. "Well," she went on, "perhaps you'd prefer the test."

"Spelling bee," a kid in the back called out.

"Neither," I said, louder than I meant to. I kicked Alicia's chair in rhythm (*dum-dum-dum-dum*).

"Each team will choose the words for their opposites," the Bird went on. "And, well, now, let's pick the captains." Alicia waved her hand in the air like she wanted to set it in orbit. "All right, Alicia, you may be one, and . . . and we'll let our other new pupil, Sammy Mott, be the other."

Alicia leaned back and smiled at me. I didn't smile back. We chose sides. Alicia picked Wally first off. "No fair," he groaned, and everybody laughed.

"People, if you're not going to settle down we'll just cancel the fun," Mrs. Bird announced.

So Alicia and me kept going till everybody was on

a team. The Bird lined us up, Alicia's fifteen kids by the windows and mine by the bulletin board.

"Captains last," Alicia ruled, and started shooting off big words at our team. We were dropping like flies with "Mercurochrome" and "noxious" and "pneumonia." I mean, a *lot* of people were messing up.

Our words for them weren't so bad either. We gave them "ludicrous," which my mom uses a lot, and "antidisestablishmentarianism," which the kid got right, if Mrs. Bird can be trusted. Really, even when people lost it wasn't awful because the words sounded so hard you had to be a genius, practically, to get them right. It was almost fun.

I thought hard about what to give Alicia. But I didn't know what words were hard to spell. Almost everything big is hard for me. Kids were saying that "antidisestablishmentarianism" wasn't really hard, and if *that* wasn't, what was? Finally, as she was standing there, waiting, I hit on the right word for Alicia. "Malocclusion," I said, thinking of the famous severe malocclusion of the upper mandibular palate.

"Malocclusion," Alicia said, remembering to say the word first.

"M-A-L . . ." She bit her lip and stared at the floor. "M-A-L-I-C-C-L-U-S-I-O-N." She looked at me. "Is that right?"

I didn't know if it was right or not.

"No, Alicia," Mrs. Bird said. "I'm afraid today *is*

unlucky for you. The word begins M-A-L-*O*, not M-A-L-*I*."

"Sammy *pronounced* it wrong," Alicia said, her voice high and wavering. She wasn't used to losing. "He gave it to me wrong."

Mrs. Bird shook her head no. "We must be good sports," she said.

"So now he has to spell it," Alicia went on. "When one person gets a word wrong, the next one has to spell it."

She was really mad at me. And I hadn't even meant anything bad by it. I didn't know it was all that hard. For all I knew there weren't *any* words she couldn't spell.

"Malocclusion, Sammy," Alicia said, her voice still raised.

"No, no, I've already let the cat out of the bag on that one," Mrs. Bird insisted. "You'll just have to think of another. I'm sure you'll think of something."

"What's the score?" Alicia asked.

"It's tied," Mrs. Bird said. "There are five left on each team, but we don't care about the score. And there are no grades. This is just for fun."

Fun, like those roller coasters that shoot backward and make you throw up. "I'm sorry," I said to Alicia.

She looked at me, startled. "Sorry?" she asked. "You're not supposed to be sorry. You're supposed to be glad. That's cute." She turned to the girl next to her, and whispered in her ear.

"A-*lish*-a," the girl said, giggling. "That's *silly*."

"All right," Alicia said to me, "I have it."

I stood there, my heart beating like the guns in war movies—*bam-bam-pow-bam-boom*. Alicia waited until everyone was listening.

"Sammy," she said, "your word is . . . 'cute.' "

Half her team groaned. The other half laughed. "Geez, Alicia," a kid complained.

My team cheered. "She gave it to us," somebody yelled.

I froze between the ears. She did it to prove how smart she is, I thought. I tried to trace the word on my jeans with my fingernail. Sometimes it helps to scratch it out and *feel* how it looks. But I had already waited too long. Everybody but the gigglers were quiet.

I couldn't remember *seeing* the word anywhere, so I tried to sound it out. "Cute," I said, and got some more laughs. "Q," I started. "Q-T, cute." I felt like a mouse caught in a spring trap.

Alicia shook her head slightly. Then she started whispering something, mouthing the letters, but all I could make out was "U."

"Q-U-T," I tried fast.

Her eyes got a queer, scared look, and she shook her head again.

"No," I corrected myself, "Q-T-U." Maybe that's what she meant.

"You cutie, you," the girl next to me shouted, breaking up.

Alicia's team cheered. Then everybody started going like a laugh track on prime-time TV. Except for Alicia they were all giggling, howling, and snickering.

I'd gotten myself out of stuff like that before. "Oh, isn't that crazy! How could I have said that? I didn't mean it." I laughed like a master of ceremonies. "She *pronounced* it wrong." But it was no-win this time. I didn't have the energy to be a clown any longer so I just sagged down at my desk.

"Well, then," Mrs. Bird broke in over the noise, "now both captains are eliminated. And that leaves five on Alicia's side and four on Sammy's. You certainly have been choosing challenging words." And they roared even louder. "People! People!" she commanded.

I didn't really know what had happened. But it was making me sick. I just got up and left the room.

"Bye, bye, cutie," I heard somebody say.

I went to the bathroom and threw up my breakfast, got my red jacket off the floor of my locker, and walked down the steps and out the side door. I didn't know where I was going, but the minute I opened the door I felt better.

I headed uptown past the travel agency and Dr. Reynolds' office. My braces still weren't wired and I could imagine my teeth easing themselves back to where they'd started out a month ago. Severely mal-occluded. With an O somewhere in the middle.

Alicia missed, too, I thought. But it didn't do much good thinking that. "Malocclusion" was like high-school hard, but "cute" was nothing. Less than noth-ing. How bad had I spelled it?

In my pocket I had a Susan B. Anthony dollar my mom had given me, so I went into Baskin-Robbins. One of the flavors looked just like I felt but I couldn't read what kind of ice cream it was.

"What's that?" I asked, pointing.

"Licorice," the guy said. "Want a taste?"

"No, thanks," I told him. "I'll have a dip of va-nilla."

"You not in school today?" he asked.

"No, I'm home sick," I told him and left, jingling the change in my pocket.

I should just light out, I thought, and hitchhike across the country. For a while I even held my thumb out to see what would happen, but nobody stopped. Then I remembered hearing Mom say that nobody would ever hire me. So how would I live? I couldn't even read the name of the street I was standing on.

The way those kids had laughed, I thought maybe

I could make a bundle on TV just spelling words wrong. I'd be a riot. Even Wally had been laughing.

I reached in my pocket to get his address so I could throw it away. I wouldn't be needing it. But it wasn't there. It wasn't *there*. I decided I must have lost it when I got the money out for the ice cream.

And then it hit me—what was really happening. I'm not even a finder anymore, I thought. I'm a loser. I lost my storm paper. I lost Wally's address. I lost the game, the fun, fun game. Maybe the whole game.

I ducked in the drugstore, stared at the caramels, and just generally hacked around until I was afraid maybe the lady who was stacking shampoo would call the police or something on me. The library was just down the street and they don't hassle you there, so I went in and headed for the Children's Room. Stacked down at the end where my mom had showed me were the Easy Books. Easy for second graders, hard for dumbheads. I saw this book I'd read in California about a bear. I could read all the words and used to like the way this baby bear wandered off and sat on a . . .

Suddenly I laughed out loud, and a lady and her kid dragging a stuffed rabbit looked at me funny. I was remembering how I had a book report due next week, my first one at this school. I just knew there'd be some kid who'd write one about a huge book on the French (Fresh) Revolution or something. And then I'd get a big whammo Sammo laugh handing mine in on *Baby Bear and the Ant Hill.*

I asked the librarian and he showed me where the archeology books were, but even looking at the titles made me feel so bad I didn't take one off the shelf. I just headed for the front door. The library has a warning system, two tall columns you walk between. If you're stealing a book, sirens go off. I was sure it would go off for me. Not for stealing books. That's the last thing I'd want to steal. It's just that I was me and I wasn't in school.

When I dashed through fast the siren didn't even whine. At least it wasn't going to tell.

The flashing lights of the bank clock down the street said *1:13* and *63° F., 17° C.* And it was raining, a steady downpour from a light gray sky. Up ahead I saw the silver canopy at my orthodontist's. Mrs. Glass had called it the Professional Building. I stood in front in the rain until I figured out that's what it said. But I wasn't sure if I knew it said Professional Building because that's how I'd sounded it out or because that's what Mrs. Glass had said it said.

I ducked under the canopy and, just by habit, climbed the steps to Dr. Reynolds' office.

"Sam Mott," I told the receptionist. "I'm here for my one o'clock appointment."

She ran her finger down her appointment calendar. "I don't have you down for one o'clock," she said. "In fact, I don't have you down for today at all."

"Can't I just wait?" I asked her. "I got out of school and all."

"I don't know where your mother got the idea you had an appointment today."

I just stood there. It was her move. "Oh, all right," she said. "We'll squeeze you in. But you'll have to wait."

I don't know why I wanted to get my teeth pulled together. Somehow I thought it might help. I wondered what Dr. Reynolds would say if I asked him to tighten the screws in my head.

But when he finally sat me down and laced me up, Dr. Reynolds did most of the talking. He told me all about how he'd come in from the hall on tornado day to find his window broken and the smile mobile blown all the way over in the sink, how he'd gotten a flat tire on the way home, and how it had been a crazy, crazy day, hadn't it?

"Og," I said.

At three o'clock I headed back to school to pick up the kids at the kindergarten door. The rain had stopped and the sky was clearing. What would have happened to them if somebody had given me a ride to Denver or New York City or someplace and I hadn't been there like I'd said? Probably nothing. They were smart kids.

I ran fast so I wouldn't have to talk to anybody I met. When I did pass a guy from my class, he yelled, "Hey, Cutes, where were you?" and tried to stop me. But I dodged past. Alicia spotted me, too, and she turned to run in my direction.

"Are you ever in trouble!" she said. "They were looking all over for you. I told the girls you probably were mad at me for giving you such a silly word and that's why you didn't spell it. I just thought it would be funny, Sam. I honestly didn't know you couldn't handle it. I thought it was easy enough. Sammy"—she grabbed my arm and we ran along together with her tugging at my sleeve—"you've really got a *problem*. Would you like me to be your tutor? I'd be very good. I expect I could work miracles."

That's all I needed. I shoved her off so she landed in the grass.

"That's all right, Sammy," she called after me as I ran. Like she *understood* me. I don't know why, but that made me even madder.

The boys were rolling in the dandelions. I herded them up and we lost Miss Priss running home. Maybe she wasn't even following.

There was a package of bran muffins and a bowl of green grapes on the kitchen table. And a printed note.

I sent the kids to let Rooster out of his basement prison and sat down with the note. It was pretty easy. It took me awhile but I could read it. Mrs. G. was learning how to write for dumbheads. She knew. Strike three, I thought. No more baby-sitting these funny kids.

"Sam," it read. "Walk the dog. Feed the kids. I want to talk to you. Mrs. Glass. P.S. Brenda left this book for you." It was a book for kids about archeology. I knew it even though I couldn't read the word on the cover. There were pictures in it like you wouldn't believe of gold masks and big stones with writing on them and a half dug-up statue. As I looked through it I saw one chapter called "Fakes." More than anything, more than *anything* I wanted to read that book all the way through like I was a brain.

"Forget the book. Let's take Rooster out," Alex said. And Chuck pushed open the door and disappeared with the dog into the backyard. I flung the book on the table and followed him.

In the backyard power saws were buzzing. On the front porch two men were fitting in new windowpanes. The place was screaming with action.

After running around the block and cleaning up after Rooster, we hurried into the backyard to watch the tree men slice branches off the maple tree and feed them into a fierce wood-grinding truck. We hung around until they told us to "get outta here or you'll get splinters in your eyes." We watched the window guys, too. "Stay back," they said. "Wouldn't want to slice you up," and then they laughed like ha-ha-ha they would, too.

I got the kids in, finally, by telling them we'd play hide and seek. They'd seek and I'd hide. While they counted to a hundred in the kitchen—skipping numbers, I could hear them—I grabbed an NFL comforter from the unmade bottom bunk. The pillow fell off the bed and in its place sat a stale marshmallow. I flung the pillow back on top of it, wondering which kid it was who was trying to hatch a petrified dinosaur egg.

Pulling the comforter over me and settling down flat next to the bed, I felt the cat step carefully over my humps and curl on top of me. It was warm and dark in my hiding place. I closed my eyes and pretended to be in a tight cocoon, like one I once saw in a movie at school. When I finally broke free, I thought, I would fly away.

I could hear them turning the place upside down looking for me. In the living room, the shower stall, closets, dresser drawers. Once when Rooster came over and started sniffing the comforter, they yanked him back.

"Rooster, you leave Al alone. He's a sleeping cat."

Before long I heard the front door open and Mrs. Glass's voice say, "I got a ride home from the office, dear hearts. Where are you?"

"Alley, alley, in come free," Chuck bellowed.

"Game's over!" Alex yelled.

"What on earth?" Mrs. Glass said.

"We can't find Sam," Alex told her.

"Can't find Sam?" she asked, sounding alarmed.

I flung off the cat, got to my feet, and staggered into the front hall, the comforter draped over my shoulders. "We were playing hide and seek," I told her. "That's why they couldn't find me. I was under the cat."

"Under Al?" she asked. "That cat's going to have to go on a good diet." She handed Alex a grocery bag. "Alex, you and Chuckie put these groceries away and set the table—fork on the left, knife and spoon on the right—and don't eat any of the cookies. Sam and I have something to talk about."

___SOME BUTTERFLY___

"Something's wrong, isn't it, Sam?" Mrs. Glass asked, peering at me like she could see behind my eyes.

"Wrong?" I asked, and waited.

"Oh, come on! Look, my kids think you're the greatest baby-sitter this side of Santa Claus. I think you're nifty, too, but I'm not sure I understand you. Maybe I should call your parents. But I think you should level with me."

"Level with you?" I asked. I flung the comforter onto the floor and, rubbing Rooster's ears, thought how funny it was my cocoon hadn't turned me into something better. Some butterfly I'd turned out to be.

"Sam Mott, you look me in the eye. I can't imagine why you're grinning like the Cheshire cat. Now, just what is it that's wrong with you? I don't want to make a big thing of it, but . . ."

There didn't seem much sense in putting it off. I wiped the grin off my face and shrugged. "I'm stupid, that's all, and you don't want me around." Then I turned around to look for my jacket so I could leave.

"You're beginning to infuriate me," she said. She flopped down in a living room chair, pointed at the sofa, and said, "Sit." Rooster and me both sat at the same time.

Mrs. G. giggled, I laughed out loud, and old Rooster, who knew he'd caused it all, got up and flashed his tail back and forth.

"This is getting us nowhere fast," Mrs. G. said, still laughing. "Clearly you're not stupid. You seem reasonably well informed, have a finely honed sense of low humor, and, good grief, I'd almost forgotten, you added the digits of our phone number in your head." She leaned forward. "You call that stupid? How did you do that? I had to do it on paper to check if you were right."

She made me sound pretty good. Nobody had ever made me sound like that before. I knew she was wrong, of course. I'd known I was dumb since at least the second grade. And the number thing was just a trick. It's easy to do. "I'm stupid because I've got these problems," I tried to explain to her.

"Problems don't make people stupid," she said.

"These do," I told her. "I can't read or write too good. I've got . . ." I looked down. If only I could just go back into my dark cocoon. ". . . In California they said I've got this thing called a learning disability." I grabbed the cat, who was wandering by, and started to pet him so I wouldn't have to look at Mrs. G.

"They want to give me some more tests Monday," I went on. The cat purred. "They want to see how dumb I really am. I'm not gonna let them. I'm not gonna take their tests."

"Ah," she said, settling back in the chair. "I thought it must be something like that. I mean, all those excuses." She picked up a little glass elephant from the table next to her and polished it on her sleeve. "My kid sister Marilyn used to make more excuses than anybody. Excuses were her life-style. She has a learning disability, too. Only it's different from yours. She has an awful time remembering what she *hears*. I mean, it's just the opposite of what you're talking about. It's hard on her. She's in high school."

"Can she read?" I asked. I couldn't see what Mrs. G. was getting at. I thought *everybody* remembered what they heard.

"She's a good reader. Reads all the time. Remembers what she reads, too. It's only when she *hears* things that she has trouble remembering them. It's crazy."

"She's crazy?"

"No, *it's* crazy. I always thought a learning disability was when you had a tough time learning things you heard."

"I don't understand."

"Neither do I. But, listen, *she* took tests. She still goes to a tutor, who helps."

"I can't even read as good as Alex," I said.

"Could you read my note today? I made it easy."

"Yeah, I could tell. You said to walk Rooster. We did. And to feed the kids. They fed themselves. And you wanted to talk to me. And about the book."

"You did read it, then."

"Yeah, well, but . . ."

"And you can write some. I've seen words you've written, though, it's true, they were wretchedly spelled."

"That's what makes me stupid."

"Don't be such an idiot," she said, standing up.

"See," I said, "you called me an idiot."

Something shattered in the kitchen. "What was that?" she yelled.

"Just a jelly jar," Alex called. "Chuckie did it."

"Leave the area," she shouted to them. "Bail out. Go to your room until I clear the kitchen."

The boys filed by on the way to their room.

"Did you cut yourselves?" she asked them.

"No," Alex said.

"He pushed me," Chuck whimpered.

They slammed the door and the living room pictures shook.

"You want me to mop it up?" I asked her.

"No," she snapped. "I'm not finished with you. First of all, forget that 'stupid' stuff. I wouldn't have asked you to sit with my kids if I'd thought you were stupid. That's rubbish. You're good with the kids. But I am worried about the reading."

"I can tell stories."

"Great," she said, "a lost art. But that's not what's worrying me. What if Chuckie had cut his foot just then?" she asked, waving her arms frantic like it had really happened. "A big bloody gash."

"I'd wrap it with a towel or something and I'd call the doctor. If he was bleeding all over the place I'd dial 911 . . . or maybe call the operator." She wasn't gonna get me on that one. I'd thought about those things. Actually my mom had made me.

"How would you find the doctor's number?"

"625-3252 (adds up to 25)," I said, showing off.

"How do you know that's the number?" she asked, like I'd made it up.

"Can we come out now?" Chuck called, sniffling.

"NO. In five minutes by your clock," she called back.

"I memorized them," I said. "The panic numbers you left me—the doctor, the hospital, your number, your husband's number. Numbers are easy."

"Sure," she said sarcastically, "numbers are easy for all us dolts. Listen, I don't know that doctor's number even yet and I've called it a thousand times." She looked up to the ceiling to think. "No, make that two thousand. OK, what about my notes? Can you really handle them?"

"I don't know," I said. "If they're short and you print them clear I can, I guess. When I see a lot of words on a page I have a hard time reading each one. I don't know."

"What if somebody calls with an important message. Can you write it down?"

She had me. "Not too good. I'll try," I started. "I can't . . . there are some words I just can't . . ."

"*Four minutes!*" Alex shouted.

She gave me a long, very serious look. "You going to take those tests to find out what you can do about it?"

The cat jumped off my lap and left me by myself. "No," I said, "I'm not."

"Four minutes, thirty seconds," Alex shouted louder.

Mrs. G. and I ran for the kitchen. The jar was on its side with the jelly holding the pieces of glass together. She scooped the whole mess up bare-handed and tossed it into the garbage can. I rolled off a couple of paper towels and lifted up the goo that was left. She got a wet towel and wiped the rest off the floor just as Alex and Chuck appeared.

"He put the forks on the right and the spoons on the left," Alex said. The kitchen doorbell rang.

"Get it, will you, Sam?" Mrs. Glass said. "I'm checking on my gracious table setting."

It was Wally. "Sam," he said, "you OK?"

I shrugged.

"I didn't know if you'd be here, for sure. I just wanted to give you my address," he went on. "I was going to give it to you after the spelling bee, but . . ."

"You mean I didn't lose it?" I asked him.

He looked at me funny. "You didn't have it to lose. Here. 724 Forest. You still coming tomorrow? Eight-thirty. I mean, is it still OK?"

"OK," I said, wondering if he was feeling sorry for me. Or if maybe he felt guilty about siccing Alicia on me after school. Maybe he would be my friend. Maybe not. "See you," I said, and closed the door.

"Friend of yours?" Mrs. Glass said, coming back in from the dining room with dollar bills in her hand.

"Wally Whiteside," I told her.

"Oh, well, then, here's your eight dollars. You can go catch up with him if you like."

"I didn't work tornado day. That's too much."

"Not true. You found the kids when I was just being hysterical. Go ahead, take it for pain and suffering."

"Is this it, then? Am I fired? If I am, it's OK," I said, but I couldn't look at her when I said it.

"I just can't decide," she told me. "If you're not going to take those tests it's as if you don't care. If you don't care about yourself, how do I know you're going to care about my kids? Let me think about it, OK?"

"OK. One more week?" I asked. "To give you time to find somebody else."

She smiled. "All right. One more week."

I *did* care. It wasn't that. I grabbed the book Brenda had left me, not that I was ever going to read it, and stuffed the bills in my pocket.

I started walking home slow, wondering if the Bird had called my folks to find out where I was. About halfway down the block, I heard Mrs. Glass yell, "Sam, oh, Sam," so I shouted back to let her know I wasn't too far to hear. "Sam, I made an appointment with your Dr. Reynolds today," she went on. "Should I be scared?"

I had to laugh out loud. I could see Mrs. G. sitting there in that tilted green chair looking up at the smile mobile and those kittens bobbing on strings.

"Brace yourself," I yelled back.

DO BANANAS CHEW GUM?

Monday was one nutty day. Even breakfast was a lot of explosions, all of them louder than snap-crackle-pop. Mom said, "Yes, you will!" and I said, "That's what you think!" and Dad said, "Don't talk to your mother like that!"

"I'll strike," I told Mom. "I'll strike and just sit there and not answer anything they ask me."

"You'll do no such thing," she boomed. "You do and they'll think you're bonkers. That'd just compound your problems."

By the time I slammed the door and left for school, I wondered why I was going at all. It would have been great just to stay home and watch old movies on TV. But my folks were still boiling about my skipping school on Friday. I'd told them I left to go to the orthodontist's, that they'd forgotten I had an appointment. My freshly wired braces proved it. Except that they figured out that new brace wires hardly ever take four and a half hours to install. So if I cut a whole day now they'd probably hire a guard to walk me every morning.

I tore down the front walk, growling to myself, and when I reached the sidewalk I looked up. There was Alicia, smiling broadly.

"Sorry again about 'cute,' " she said cheerfully. "I didn't mean that to happen. I thought you could spell it."

"Yeah, well, you don't have my head." Maybe she *hadn't* meant it. I wasn't sure. How can you tell about people?

"You want to help?" she asked, and shoved a big box at me. It smelled like a bakery. "There's too much for me to carry."

I took it like an idiot.

"Today's my birthday," she announced, walking backward in front of me. What could I do? I followed her. "I'm twelve. Daddy says I should write a book while I'm twelve and people will pay a lot of attention because I'm so young. But I can't think of anything to write about. Got any ideas?"

"What's in this box?" I asked, holding it out to her. "I can't carry it much longer. I'm in a hurry."

"Cupcakes. Birthday cupcakes. They have my initials on them. All except one."

"You going to a party or something?"

"I'm giving them out after lunch. Mrs. Bird said I could. I have napkins, too, with red and blue cornflowers on them. The initials are in red. Want to look?"

"No," I told her, "I hate cupcakes." We were only a couple of blocks from school and up ahead I could see kids I knew. I had to get away from Alicia fast, but first there was something I'd been thinking about. "Listen, those girls said you told them about me. Remember? Before class Friday? What did you tell them? Did you tell them I can't spell and that I'm dumb and everything?"

"Oh, no," she said, looking shocked at the idea. "I told them you kissed me when we were in the trash room."

I stopped dead. "Geez, Alicia. I don't believe you."

"Sure," she went on. "They were very interested. Nobody had ever kissed them."

It was so nutty I could have smacked her over the head with the cupcake box.

"Well, you just take it back," I yelled. "It's a lie. I didn't even *want* to. Besides, it won't do you any good to have me as your boyfriend. I'm a dumbhead and you know it and they want to give me tests today so pretty soon everybody else will know it, too." I pushed the cupcake box back at her and she had to drop her books to grab it.

"What kind of tests?" she asked, cocking her head at me.

"Tests. I don't know."

"I like to take tests."

"I don't. I'm not going to, either."

"That would be silly. Do you think you'll get to see the psychologist and take those tests with ink blots?"

"I'm not going to see anybody. I'm not going to take any tests." Suddenly I felt like I was Chuck sitting under the table saying, "I don't take pills." And I remembered how he closed his eyes and opened his mouth and did it anyway. I wondered if that was smart of him or not.

"Well, if you're not off taking tests, you can come to my party in class. I don't care if you're not smart."

I thought maybe Alicia wasn't so bad after all. Or maybe she didn't care because she thought she was smart enough for both of us. She opened up the box and showed me the rows of cupcakes.

"I made them myself. From a mix." They were iced white, with red icing letters on them that said AB, AB, AB, AB. All except one. It said SAM. I tried to take it out to pitch it, but she zapped the lid on my fingers.

Two girls ran up to join her. "Hi, Alicia, hi, Cutes," they said.

I slunched over and stalked off to school. "Don't leave because of uh-us," one of them sang after me.

On the playground Wally was showing his fossil to a whole huddle of guys. He'd found a great little fern that had been hiding in its rock for thousands of years.

He was the only one who'd found anything. We'd had a good time looking, though. Really.

But I was sure if I went over to talk to Wally, somebody was bound to call me names because of Friday. If I stayed where I was, Alicia and the girls would catch up with me. If I left the class to take tests, people would guess where I was. If I stayed in class, I'd have to get a cupcake with SAM on it and tell the Bird what I was going to do my science report on when I didn't know from beans. Too many ifs. Ifs multiplied by ifs. I had to make up my mind.

I dodged inside, away from both Wally and Alicia, hurried past the principal's office, and dashed up the stairs. At least it was quiet up there so I could think and the Bird wasn't going to call me names.

I tossed my jacket in the locker and took a deep breath. I decided to close my eyes and let them throw in the pill. It had to be worse to stay *in* class than to leave.

I opened the door and marched up to Mrs. Bird.

"I'm sorry about Friday," I told her, feeling like an apologizing machine. That made it two days in a row.

"So am I," she said. "Your parents said you went to the orthodontist?" she asked.

"I'm going to do it," I shouted at her. "I'm going to take the tests."

She looked totally confused. Maybe she thought I was going to all along. She didn't even know about the ifs. "I know," she said, "at nine-thirty." She fussed around with the stuff on her desk and pointed to her calendar. *Sammy*, it said on it, *9:30.*

"You can scoot off to room 102 right after current events."

I sank down in my desk, opened the top, and tried to straighten up the mess inside. When people came in I guess I looked like I was busy and not interested in talking. They left me alone.

By the time current events was over and kids had stood up and read their clippings about the earthquake in Japan and the elections and energy problems and the guy who'd robbed the Laundromat downtown, my hands were sweating. I'd almost decided to change my mind. If only I could neither stay nor go.

"So now let's talk about how your science reports are progressing," Mrs. Bird began. "How many plan to give them orally?" I raised my hand. No way I wanted to write it. "Oral reports must, of course, include a written bibliography and outline. And . . . oh, Sammy," she went on, "it's time for your appointment." I got up and left the room. Nobody seemed to notice or care. (Is that worse than their calling me names? I wondered.)

I trudged down to room 102. It looked like a closet from the outside, mostly because it didn't have a window like the rest of the doors did. I knocked. Very lightly, so whoever was inside wouldn't hear.

"Come in. Come in," a voice called out.

I opened the door slowly and saw that it was a little room, not closet-sized, but little, painted green like the garbage room. There was a desk, a few chairs, and a crescent-shaped table, yellow-green like a slice of honeydew melon. The lady inside said hello. She was standing up and she was almost as tall as my dad. Her face was round and shiny and she had lots of curly dark hair.

"I know you," I told her, and without even checking my dragon ring, I stuck out my hand. She shook it with both of hers.

"My name is Ms. Huggins," she said.

I did know her. She was always stopping in our room and talking to kids or to Mrs. Bird. I didn't know she was the learning disabilities person, though. That really knocked me out. I mean, she was at school *all* the time. That had to mean there were a *lot* of dumb kids like me. She let me sit down at the crescent table.

"Well, Sammy," she said, smiling, like she was tickled to death I'd decided to come.

"My name is Sam," I told her. Somehow I didn't want Ms. Huggins calling me the wrong name.

"OK, Sam," she said. "We've a job to do. I'm going to give you some tests today and again next Monday to find out how you learn best."

"That's what my dad said." I shrugged and stared

down at the green floor. Green tile. It was very dull. "I don't know what else you need to know," I said, like I couldn't care less. I mean, she was nice and I really didn't want her to find out more about me.

"I expect you know more about yourself than anybody else," she said. "We can start there." She sat down in a chair across from me. "What do you do best, Sam?"

"Me?" I looked up. What a stupid question, I thought. Do *best*? "I don't know. Make people laugh at me, I guess. I'm good at that."

"You mean jokes? Like 'Why did the robber take a shower at the bank?' "

"Because he wanted to make a clean getaway," I flipped back. "No, mostly not jokes. Mostly *at* me." I shrugged again, like, of course, I didn't care.

"Come on, Sam. Mrs. Bird tells me you have a special ability in math. She says you're a bright boy."

"I light up the night."

"Ah, you're a sit-down comic. Then they *do* laugh because you want them to, sometimes. How about the math?"

"I know a few tricks with numbers, that's all. I'm mostly dumb."

She laughed. Laughed. I could have punched her. She wasn't so nice after all. "No, it can't be that easy," she went on, still looking much too cheerful. "You're not allowed in my door unless you're smart. Children with a low ability level don't come to me. There's another teacher who works with them."

She'd change her mind soon enough. I wasn't going to argue with her. I'd just let her start the tests. That'd show her. I stared out the window while she got some books and paper out, wondering just *how* smart people were different from me. I tried to imagine what was in their heads that wasn't in mine.

"I'm going to ask you some crazy questions, Sam," she said.

I looked up at her, wondering what she could ask that was crazy, and why.

"First," she said, "do bananas chew gum?"

I laughed out loud. "Are you kidding?"

"Not at all," she said. "Do clocks swim?"

"No, but time flies." Mom was always big on riddles. Were these riddles that I wasn't smart enough to figure out?

"Do babies cry?"

That wasn't a trick. "Sometimes."

But then they started getting harder. After a while it was stuff like "Do interpreters translate?" Pretty soon the only word that made sense was "Do." I had to keep saying, "I don't know," and feeling like an idiot. But just when they were getting so hard I bet *she* didn't even know the answers, we started on something completely different.

Lots of pictures. You had to match them. Like this

one I remember that had a baseball on one side of the page and on the other side pictures of a violin bow, a rake, and a baseball bat. Really simp stuff. But they got harder, too.

Pretty much every new part started out easy and got hard like that. There were lots of different kinds of things, like when Ms. Huggins laid these tiles down on a table and all the tiles had weird lines on them and squiggles and she'd say, "Which shape is different from the rest?" or she'd put up another and say, "Find this shape. It's hidden in that picture." She was timing all this stuff with a stopwatch, and it was hard.

Then I was supposed to copy circles and arrows and boxes and stars and, boy, did I stink at that. So when we finally got to some math, it was like a vacation, or at least recess. It was real 2 plus 2 stuff to begin with. Then it got to be 5 1/3 times 2 1/5 equals, and then long division with decimals. She only gave me ten minutes to get it all done, but before the time was nearly up I got to these questions I didn't even know what they meant.

"That's OK," she said, "you won't learn how to do those problems until seventh grade. I knew we'd get to something you do really well. You were terrific at the math. Fast, accurate, all those good things. I doubt there's anyone in your class who could do so well."

"Alicia," I told her.

"Don't know her."

"You wouldn't."

"She pretty good at math?"

"She's good at everything. A brain." My stomach felt like lunchtime was getting close. I didn't want to start any more tests. I decided to stall. "Why is it easy for me to do math and not reading?" I asked her, even though I knew the answer. (*Dum-dum-dum.*)

She shook her head. "I'm not sure. Nobody's sure. Did you know some people can hardly do math at all? Some people just blink their eyes and shake their heads when you say that 4 plus 15 is 19. It's as if they've got a short circuit in their heads and they can't put numbers through their brain computer. If they're smart otherwise, that's a learning disability, too."

"Can they read?"

"Sometimes. Sometimes not. Learning disabilities come in all varieties."

"Like ice cream."

"More even than that." She smiled, like she knew I was stalling. "Ready for another test?"

"No," I said. "Is it hard?"

"I think so. Yes. This one's spelling."

"Yuck. Isn't it time for lunch?"

She checked her watch. "Eleven-ten. Not quite. Just this last one, OK? Then we'll break for lunch."

But geez, it was awful. After "dog" and "cat" and "hat" to make me feel like it wasn't going to be all that bad, it was word after word after word I couldn't spell

145

and I knew I was guessing wrong. At least she didn't ask me to spell "cute."

"Try sounding it out," she'd say. "Try it out loud. Keep plugging." But how do you keep plugging on "similar" and "license" and "miracle" when you hardly know how to begin? I didn't care if I *ever* knew how to spell them. I mean, who cares, anyway? Every word more I sank lower and lower in the chair. My stomach growled like a mad dog.

After I guess she figured she'd tortured me enough, Ms. Huggins beamed out this huge smile even though I knew there wasn't anything to grin about. "Cheer up," she said. "It's chow time."

I didn't smile back.

"You're doing fine. I'm finding out a lot about how you can learn even better. And the math was fabulous."

"That's me, fabulous Sam." What a fake she is, I decided. Always smiling and saying "terrific" when what she means is dumb. I get mad at Mom but at least she knows dumb when she sees it and doesn't lie about it.

"Do I have to come back?"

"Around one-thirty," she said, "we'll start afresh. Why don't you go early to the cafeteria and take a long lunch hour. I'll give you a note. I think I hear a hungry monster in your stomach."

It wasn't funny, so I didn't pretend it was. I just stared at her.

While she wrote out the pink permission slip I got up and hung around the door.

"See you at one-thirty," she said, holding out the paper. "Right after the party."

I started to bolt out the door. "Party?"

"Didn't Mrs. Bird say there'd be a party after lunch?"

"Oh, yeah," I said, remembering. "There'll be a bunch of bananas hanging around up there chewing gum and eating cupcakes." And I slammed the door on her silly smile.

11

WHY NOT SAM MOTT?

THE LUNCH HOUR went on forever. We had pizza cas-
serole. Not many kids like it so an awful lot got
smashed up in the trash compacter. I threw away about
half of mine, even though I'll eat almost anything. If
Wally lost his retainer in stuff like that, I'd refuse to
look for it. Or maybe I wouldn't. If he was still my
friend.

After lunch I sat by myself, watched the first graders
play, and then poked around in the grass with a stick,
pretending to dig up treasures. All I found was a rusty
nail and a few ants, who crawled all over a cookie
crumb I fed them.

When the bell rang there wasn't anything to do but
go back inside with the big stream of kids, like I was a
fish on a hook. And there wasn't anything inside I
wanted to do.

Mrs. Bird's room was all laughs and giggles. It
sounded so happy when I slammed my locker door I

wondered if maybe it wouldn't be a great party after all. I was the last kid in, but Mrs. Bird hadn't gotten back from her lunch yet.

"Cutie," a girl yelled. "Did you see your cupcake yet?" I looked around the room, and on every desk was a cupcake, a napkin, and a paper cup with something in it. But kids were gathered around my desk like the ants on the crumb.

"Mine has AB on it for the birthday girl. What does it say on yours, Cutes?" a boy asked with a smirk.

"How do you *spell* it?" somebody giggled. They were really starting to laugh at me.

And I got mad. I got so mad I could have zapped them. I *know* getting mad makes it worse, but I could feel my face get red and I felt like I could level them all. I straight-armed the guy nearest me. Alicia just stood there by her desk and looked confused. It was like she knew she kept botching me up and didn't understand how.

The stupid cupcake sat there. SAM was on it with a red heart iced around the letters. I hadn't even noticed *that* before.

"What does it *say*?" somebody in the back asked. "Does it really say 'cute'?"

I picked up the cupcake and held it up high for them to see. I shouted so everyone could hear, "It says Sam. That's my name. I don't want to be called anything else. And don't you forget it." They looked at me with their mouths open and I stared them down, feeling tall like a statue.

I would have kept talking, too, but Mrs. Bird came back. She stood at the door of the silent room, trying to decide what was going on. Her eyes fixed on me.

"Sammy," she called out. I didn't move. I just got madder. "Sammy," she went on, "were you screaming? I could hear you down the hall."

"I was saying," I told her in less than a shout, "that my name is Sam. And I don't want to be called Sammy or New Kid or Metal Mouth or Dumbhead or—especially—Cutes. I don't want to be called anything but Sam Mott."

"That sounds reasonable to me," she said mildly. "Everybody agree to that?"

There was a kind of general mumbling and I sat down in my seat, feeling like a balloon somebody had let the air out of—like I had been all filled up with being mad and now it was gone I just felt bad. Mrs. Bird just didn't understand. I ate the top off the cupcake. The room was still very quiet.

"That was really something," Wally whispered.

I nodded, my mouth full of sweet stuff. Gulping it down, I said, "I was mad."

"Yeah," he said, "I could tell."

We all had to sing "Happy Birthday" to Alicia. And I sang it like almost everybody else did, "Happy birthday to you, you belong in a zoo. You look like a monkey, and you smell like one, too." I mean, that's the way we *always* sang it. There'd been about four birthdays since I'd been in this school and mostly everybody sang it that way. It wasn't being mean to Alicia, like name calling. After my big speech it worried me some. But I don't think it was. She didn't look mad.

After we finished eating the cupcakes and drinking lemonade, the Bird gave all the captains math problems to pass back. Then she stopped at my desk and leaned over. "Are you all right?" she asked and I nodded. "You may be excused, Sam," she said. "I would have called you Sam sooner if I'd known."

"Oh, it wasn't just you," I told her, and hurried out of the room while almost everybody else was groaning over the math.

I knocked on the door of room 102.

"Come in. Come in," Ms. Huggins called like before. When I opened it, she said, "You're back!" like she was surprised but glad. "How's the monster in your stomach?"

"Just fed him a cupcake and he's happy," I told her. I didn't know why I wasn't mad at her anymore.

We started out with easy stuff. Numbers.

"Repeat after me," she said, "17-1-4-42." Stuff like that. And it wasn't hard at all. A piece of cake. A piece of *cup*cake.

"Do you see?" she asked me when the test was over.

"Do you see how much easier it is for you to learn from what you *hear* than from what you read? You remembered those so well."

The test had seemed easy. I did see, sort of.

"You don't have to read things to learn them," she went on. "Most people learn a lot by listening to other people, to movies, to television. You can even learn to *read* better by listening to *yourself*."

That sounded crazy. "How?"

"Just say there's a word you want to read . . ." she started.

"There *is*," I told her. "There is!" I'd stuck the archeology book Brenda had left for me in the orange crate with my good junk. I'd looked through it and even read a little bit of it. But I still couldn't figure out the word on the cover. I was sure it must be "archeology."

"Archeology," I said, almost begging. "That's the word I want to read. Can you teach me that one?"

"Good grief, you start at the top, don't you?" She wrote the word down for me on a piece of white paper, kind of splitting it up into parts—ARC-HE-OL-O-GY. "It isn't the easiest word to sound out, but . . ."

Then she took another piece of paper and tore a little square hole out of the middle. She put the hole on the word so I could just see the first three letters and she made me sound it out. Twice. And I did it. She moved the paper and I sounded out all the parts.

Then she had me do that about ten times before she let me look at the word whole. And I could sound it out. Arc-he-ol-o-gy. Archeology. I kept looking at the word and saying it over. Out loud. Archeology. I was so excited I felt dizzy.

"Can I have the paper with the hole?"

"My compliments. But it's not magic. You've got to do the work."

Then I looked at the paper and wondered how many words in the new book I could do that way by myself. But she kept after me. "Sam, that was terrific! The computer in your head sometimes gets confused by a lot of letters. If you just let it see a few at a time for a while, it'll help.

"There are so many things you can do, Sam. Have somebody record the pages you have to read, then listen to the tape as you read the words to yourself. Then try making a tape of your voice reading the words. Can you do that?"

"No kidding?" I asked her. "A tape recorder? It would be OK? My mom said it would be a crutch."

"Nothing's wrong with a crutch if you need one. If you had a broken leg she'd let you have a crutch. If you've got a tape recorder, put it on your desk to take notes for you. I'll talk to Mrs. Bird about it. Reporters take notes with tape recorders all the time."

"I'm earning the money for one right now!" I'd tell Mrs. Glass and she'd let me stay. I was sure she would.

Then we started another test and I had to guess which of a list of words fit best into paragraphs that were hard to read and I felt awful again.

"This would be easy for Alicia and Wally," I told Ms. Huggins. "It's not fair."

"Right," she said, "it's not. Wouldn't be fair if you fell off your bike and broke your elbow either, but you'd have to deal with it, fair or not. You can either give up and just plug your head into a TV set or you can work like crazy. I can help. Your folks can help. A lot of people can help. But in the end it's got to be you."

Then she gave me another test. There was this one word at the top and five words listed under it. I was supposed to find the word that meant nearly the same as the word at the top. Like there'd be "nap" and under it would be "jump," "roll," "bad," and "sleep." Ms. Huggins said if I couldn't decide which word fit best to just go on to the next question. After the first four or five I was a disaster.

"You'll get there, Sam," she said when I started sagging down in my chair.

"Never," I groaned.

"Listen," she told me, still cheerful like I was winning the race, not crawling along on my knees, "Thomas Edison had a learning disability in school, and so did Hans Christian Andersen, and Vice President Rockefeller, and President Wilson. They didn't get famous by saying 'never.' They worked their way out of it. You can, too, but you have to do it a step at a time. Nobody's going to wave a wand."

When I left room 102 I felt better. Some. "We'll find out more about you next Monday, Sam Mott," she said. "After that we'll work together several times a week." It was like I'd just waded up to my ankles in cold Lake Michigan water knowing I had to swim across the lake and back again.

The bell rang to go home. It had been a long afternoon, a long day. But it was Monday and I didn't have Chuck and Alex to play with. The day was sunny and warm so I just wandered outside, leaving my jacket up in my locker. Just watch it snow tomorrow, I thought. But I didn't care.

Alicia was standing at the corner by the crossing guard. And I was glad to see her. I really was.

"Hey, Alicia," I called.

She turned around and walked back slow, like she was afraid of what I was going to do. "You were really mad at me," she said.

"No," I told her. "Not exactly." What I wanted to do was tell her about the afternoon. That other stuff didn't matter now. "I just took some tests. There weren't any ink blots."

"You're not mad at me?" she said.

"If I was, I'm not anymore." The crossing guard held up his stop sign to the traffic and we crossed over with the crowd of waiting kids. On the other side she opened up the big cupcake box. It was empty except for one. "Sandy was absent," she said. She broke it into two pieces and gave me half. "If there weren't any ink blots, what were there, then?" she asked.

"Well," I told her, my mouth full of icing, "the first question was 'Do bananas chew gum?' "

She laughed. "Were they trying to find out if you're crazy?"

"I don't think so. It was more like true-false to tell if I could understand what I hear. Another one was 'Do reptiles slither?' "

"What did they *say*, though—about you?"

"It was Ms. Huggins who gave me the tests," I told her. "You know, the tall lady who smiles. She said I'm not dumb."

"I never thought you were. Look, Sam, you told me to stop telling everybody about being so smart. And I am. Trying to stop, I mean. I think you better just stop talking about being dumb."

"Maybe," I shrugged. "But reading and writing like I do seems dumb to me." We started walking and it didn't seem so crazy to be talking to Alicia. She seemed like my friend. I turned to her and said, "Ms. Huggins told me about all these famous guys, like Edison and President Wilson and all, who had learning disabilities like I do when they were kids. They all had a hard time in school, but look what they did. At least that's what she said."

"If they can do it, why not Sam Mott?" Alicia asked. "Why not?"

"Why not? I mean, maybe I'll be a ditch digger or something I don't need to read a lot for. Maybe, though," I told her, "I'll dig up gold and silver statues and skeletons and broken pots and Viking helmets and swords and garbage pits and all. And then I'll tell people what it all means. Is that crazy?"

"No crazier than me saying I'm going to be a psychiatrist," she said. "Somehow I don't think understanding people is what I do best. Maybe I should just discover an alternate energy source."

"I think," I told her, "I'll do my science report on archeology. Will you read some stuff with me?"

"Why not?" she said.

As soon as I got home I called Mrs. Glass to ask her if I could borrow the things we'd dug up from the tree roots to use for my school report and to tell her I'd taken the tests.

She laughed. No, she hooted. "Sam, I knew you'd do it. I really knew. I hated myself for threatening you, but if that had anything to do with your finally taking them, I'm glad I did it." Then she paused. "As for the great tree treasure, I don't have it anymore."

"Don't have it?" She'd dumped it. I knew it. It was

all dirty so she'd just tossed it in the garbage. "Did you really throw it away?" I asked her. "All that stuff? *All of it?*"

"Oh, not all of it," she said. "Come on, Sam, now who's calling who dumb?" And she kind of giggled. "I took it over to the Historical Society on Saturday. They're going to devote one whole display case to our tornado wonders. But you can borrow what you want for your report.

"Look, Chuckie and Alex and I will take you over right now. It's a pretty impressive place. They let me write the labels for our display," she said. "And there's one I especially want you to see. You know what I wrote on the label for the tapping gouge?"

"Uh, 'This is a tapping gouge'?" I guessed.

"Come on. I wrote—tell me what you think of it— 'Found in the roots of a sugar maple tree by archeologist Sam Mott, age twelve.'"

I dug in my pocket and got out the word Ms. Huggins had written. "Arc-he-ol-o-gy." I could still read it. Over the telephone I could hear Rooster barking.

"Chuckie," Mrs. Glass called away from the phone, "you and Alex get your jackets. We're going to pick up Sam."

I felt like somebody had poured a gallon of pop over me, not the wet, just the bubbles. Archeologist, Sam Mott, age twelve.

"I can *read* that," I said.

JAMIE GILSON's previous novels have earned widespread praise for their rich characterization, dialogue, and humor. *Harvey, the Beer Can King*, the author's first, received a juvenile book award from the Friends of American Writers. Of *Dial Leroi Rupert, DJ, School Library Journal* said, "Characters of all ranks are well drawn, and Gilson has an eye for details . . . a contemporary story both amusing and suspensefully told."

Ms. Gilson, a former junior high school teacher and radio, television, and film writer/producer, is a freelance writer for *Chicago* magazine, conducts creative writing workshops, and lectures frequently on several of her favorite topics: the Vikings, the Pilgrims, colonial America, and cave paintings. She, her husband, Jerome, a trademark lawyer, and their three children live in Wilmette, Illinois.